7

ec
e

Г
(01
N
(
N
(

# OUT OF THE BLUE

**By the same author:**
*Blood Ties*, The Book Guild, 2003

# OUT OF THE BLUE

Daniel Peltz

The Book Guild Ltd
Sussex, England

First published in Great Britain in 2004 by
The Book Guild Ltd
25 High Street
Lewes, East Sussex
BN7 2LU

Typesetting in Baskerville by
Acorn Bookwork, Salisbury, Wiltshire

Printed in Great Britain by
Antony Rowe Ltd, Chippenham, Wiltshire

A catalogue record for this book is available from
The British Library.

ISBN 1 85776 814 0

*For my parents*

# Acknowledgements

My thanks to: Elizabeth Peltz, Laura Townsley, Paul Phillips and Nicky Burns

# PART ONE

## London: October 2002

### The Arrival

# 1

Candice drove the short distance from her home in Eaton Square to Kensington Court. The rain was falling more heavily now than at any time during the day. As she got out of the car, she rushed to the boot and hurriedly snatched her medical bag and umbrella. Closing the boot she then locked the car with her remote-control key, and pushed open the umbrella. Relaxing a little more, now that she was protected from the pouring rain, she recovered her poise and walked to the entrance of Kensington Court, the block of flats where her patient, Madame Bromberg lived.

The buzzer sounded, and Candice pulled the door open, and then walked towards the old-fashioned lift at the end of the dimly lit hallway. She opened the lift door, pulled back the grill, and pushed the button marked 'six'.

As the lift groaned its way up to the sixth floor Candice began to concentrate on her old and terminally ill patient. Under twenty-four-hour care, Madame Bromberg was fast running out of resistance. Throughout her adult life she had hardly lost a day to illness. However, over the last three months, the cancer that had first taken hold in her stomach had now remorselessly spread to other parts of her body. The pain was at times unbearable. Death would come as a welcome relief to her.

# 2

"Allo, Marianna, *ça va?*" Candice asked as she walked into the small one-bedroom flat.

"Oh please don't talk to me in French. We agreed on that ... *ça va?*! How can I be *ça va?* I'm in terrible pain and I'm dying ... ouch! Be careful, woman! See, Candice – see how rough she is." The old lady pointed at the nurse.

Candice smiled sympathetically at the nurse. She then looked back at her patient. "What I meant was, are you feeling all right. I know that you are sick." Candice felt stupid. It was one of those remarks that she would normally ask her patients, to which they would usually respond in a positive way. However, knowing Marianna Bromberg and the kind of person she was, the question was absurd. Racked with pain, and in permanent discomfort, the old woman's response was more than predictable. She decided to move on.

"Marianna, come on, you are not usually this upset." Candice was kneeling down beside her patient, stroking the wrinkled but tender cheek of the old woman.

"Oh I don't know. I just want it to be over. I've had enough. Candice, please help me."

Candice looked at her, tears beginning to well up in her eyes. This extraordinary woman, who was so phlegmatic when it came to complaining about her illness, was now finally cracking up under the strain.

"I can't do any more. You have to take the drugs. It will help the pain go away." Candice turned her head back towards the nurse.

"Listen to the doctor, Madame. You must take your pills." The nurse walked towards the old woman with her medication, which she had refused to take earlier.

Having swallowed the various tablets, Madame Bromberg noticeably relaxed. Candice stood up and walked back to the chair facing her.

"Would you excuse us?" Madame Bromberg asked the nurse to leave. "I need to talk to the doctor alone."

Candice nodded at the nurse, who abruptly left the room. "You should be a little more polite to her, Marianna. She's only doing her job.

"Ach! She is stupid, and a busybody. I don't need her ... well, I wouldn't if you came more often to give me my pills."

"That's impossible, and you know it. Marianna, be reasonable."

"I will try, but I can't promise." She smiled mischievously at Candice. "I have something to tell you!"

"Well? What is it, then? You have my undivided attention." Candice responded.

"It's arrived."

"What?"

"Look!" Madame Bromberg lifted her arm and pointed towards the half-opened brown package resting against the wall, next to the front door.

"My God! When did it come? It must have been right out of the blue!" Candice said, looking at the package.

The two women looked at each other and began to laugh.

# PART TWO

## Paris: July 1942

### The Velodrome

# 1

Living in a spacious and elegant apartment on the fourth floor on the Avenue Henri Martin, the Brombergs in normal circumstances would have been considered a successful and privileged family. However these were not normal times. As prominent Jews, the family was totally exposed to the evil force that had suffocated France's capital at that time.

The Nazi occupation of Paris had meant that Daniel Bromberg would have to change all of his future plans. Having studied art history at the Sorbonne, Daniel borrowed from his father, a successful fur trader, enough money to set up an art gallery in the Faubourg St Honoré. Through the large network of friends that he had made at university, he managed to meet a number of young artists at the cutting edge of the vibrant Paris art market in the second decade of the century.

It was only a matter of time before he had made a name for himself, at first by exhibiting the work of well-established artists such as Cézanne, Degas and Sisley. He immediately began to attract a rich and distinguished clientele, desperate to cash in on the explosion of talent which over the past few decades had transformed the very principles of art itself. By the mid-twenties Daniel Bromberg was arguably the premier art dealer in Paris, not only handling the Impressionists and Post-Impressionists, but also trading in the work of younger greats such as Picasso, Braque and Duchamp. No major work was bought or sold without Daniel Bromberg knowing about it, or being involved.

# 2

It was at this time, when Daniel had just turned thirty that he met a young woman who happened to be bidding for a painting, which he himself was eager to buy for an even more eager client. At first he took little notice, but then became quite irritated by the aggressive style of the young woman's bidding. This irritation soon turned to anger as she refused to concede. Daniel was certainly not used to being outbid on the floor, particularly at this time, when he was so well known and was acting for all of the wealthiest and most established art collectors in the French capital.

The loss of the painting, a mediocre Renoir, did not upset him as much as the fact that his ego had been punctured by an unknown woman who had the audacity to bid so aggressively against him. Bidding against him was bad enough, but losing to her was far too much for the arrogant hotshot art dealer. He was not going to let her leave the room without finding out more about her.

"Excuse me ... Can I ask you why you were so keen to buy it? It is, after all, nothing special. If you wanted a good Renoir, you should have bid for lot thirty-two," he said to her, walking out of the sales room.

"Do I know you?" the young woman asked him, turning around, stopping at the doorway and ignoring his question.

Daniel began to stutter. The young woman, tall, elegantly dressed in a dark brown suit, was staring at him. He felt that she was not just looking at him but looking right through him. She was certainly not beautiful in a classical sense, but she nevertheless intrigued Daniel. Her hair was tightly tied back, tucked underneath her hat. Her face revealed strong angular features, with very full lips, which were made even more pronounced by the bright red lipstick.

"I ... I ... I'm sorry, my name is Daniel ... Daniel Bromberg."

"Well, Daniel, I am Esther Rosenberg. The reason why I bought the painting was that my client liked it. There is very little more I can say. You are indeed right that lot thirty-two is a finer piece, but my client wanted this one."

"Yes but..." Daniel had effectively run out of things to say. He desperately tried to think of something to keep her attention. She began to walk away, fully expecting him to try and continue the conversation. Daniel might have been one of the leading art dealers in Paris, and he was certainly very highly regarded in the auction rooms, but as far as meeting, let alone having relationships with women were concerned, he was woefully short of experience. Esther knew that the young man, who was now walking rather quickly behind her, was smitten. If this had been a game of cards, Daniel had already revealed his entire hand without being asked! Esther meanwhile continued to hold hers close to her chest.

"Does your client live in Paris?" Daniel asked, finally thinking of a question.

"Surely you know that I cannot breach a confidence like that ... Now, please I must go. I have other appointments to get to. It's been nice meeting you."

11

Esther carried on walking outside the building, and called for a taxi. Daniel chased after her. He had never felt this way before, so invigorated, almost electrified.

"I must see you again. Please let me take you out for lunch. Do you have a card with your telephone number?"

She looked at him. He was so intense. To Daniel it seemed like an age before she responded by reaching into her handbag and pulling out with her gloved fingers a small white card.

"I look forward to meeting you again. Driver, Avenue Montaigne!"

Daniel looked down at the card that he had been given as the taxi moved away, his thumb softly stroking the raised letterhead. Although he had never really experienced anything like this before, he knew that he had fallen in love.

# 3

The courtship rapidly developed, and within a year Daniel and Esther were married. Among the Orthodox Jewish community in Paris, the wedding was one of the highlights of that warm summer of 1927. The speed at which the two of them were married had, however, raised a few eyebrows, particularly among the older women in both families. Indeed it did not take long for the gossipmongers to get what they wanted, when Daniel announced his wife's pregnancy weeks after the wedding. It wasn't the fact that Esther was pregnant that caused the consternation, but the due date of the impending arrival. First the fingers came out, as the old ladies began to count the months, and then the gasps and sniggering filtered through as it became quite clear why the wedding had taken place with such haste.

The young couple, although hurt by the gossip and disapproving remarks, comfortably rode the minor storm of embarrassment. They were not going to let the more opinionated and narrow-minded members of the families ruin their happiness. In time things returned to normal, but the Brombergs did not forget their quasi-ostracism, and would not forget the behaviour of many members of their respective families.

Marianna was born a week early, on the 3rd March 1928.

With both parents working, she was brought up by a succession of nannies. The little girl only really saw her mother and father early in the morning, or just before she went to bed in the evening. However, this lack of daytime contact did not affect her relationship with either of them. Indeed, it was quite the opposite. Having no other children, both parents doted on their daughter, providing her love, affection and security.

# 4

Nine years later, in the autumn of 1937 the Brombergs moved apartments to Avenue Henri

Martin. The flat he chose, on the fourth floor, was one of the largest in the prestigious block, located in arguably one of the finest residential streets in Paris. Reaching the apogee of his career, Daniel wanted to live somewhere that would not only reflect his towering business reputation and success, but also a place that could house his burgeoning personal collection of art.

"How many have you got to hang?" Esther asked her husband as the deliveries kept on coming in.

"Oh, don't worry ... I think this is the last one." He said, slightly apologetically.

"Are they all Picassos?"

"Yes." He responded looking at all the pictures, which were now laid on the floor against every wall.

"Couldn't you have had a little more imagination, Daniel? I mean, you do deal in all the great artists. Why only Picasso?"

"Esther, you are right. Maybe I should have varied my collection, but..."

"One other artist would have been nice!".

"As I was saying." Daniel returned to his explanation, ignoring his wife's wry sarcasm. "I could have collected other artists, but I feel there is something special ... even magical in his work. Don't you see it?" Daniel asked, pointing to the works of art in front of them.

"Yes, of course I see it. The man is a genius. It would not be an exaggeration to call him the Shakespeare of modern art. But I am just saying there are other artists. It would have been nice to have some variation." Esther was now walking ahead of her husband into the other rooms, looking at all the pieces that her husband had collected over the last five years. Of course she knew that he had been

14

collecting, and that he had always loved Picasso, but she was slightly taken aback by the number and the quality of works that he had amassed over the years and had kept at the gallery.

"What's this?" She called out, looking at a relatively small brown package resting on its own in the drawing room next to the fireplace.

Daniel followed her into the room, looked at the package, and smiled.

"Open it and see."

Esther moved slowly towards the package, and slowly began to unwrap the brown paper. She then removed the protective cardboard covering, which was sealed at the back, finally turning the painting around. She stood back and looked at the image in bewilderment. At last, after what seemed like an eternity, she managed to say something.

"My God ... where did you get it from?"


# 5


Esther walked towards the painting, and studied the picture of a young emaciated beggar crouched with a bowl in the gutter. The work, like all of his paintings during that time, was of a dark, oppressive blue. The monochrome painting, with its lonely image exhibiting elongated proportions and angular expressions was typical of this type of work. The style was melancholic yet euphoric, simple yet incredibly technical in its approach to both space and form.

"When did you buy it? Why didn't you tell me?"

"I didn't buy it. It was left to me by my oldest client, Jacques Lafarge, last year in his will. He had bought a number of Picasso Blue paintings just after the Vollard exhibition at the start of the century. Times were difficult during that period for the artist. He was struggling to survive. Jacques saw this as an opportunity and agreed to buy some. In fact, in this particular case, I think Picasso gave him the painting as a gift for helping him when times were not so good. In the codicil, it makes the proviso that I must never sell it."

"But why did he give it to you?"

"I have looked after him for fifteen years, buying and selling his collection. We were good friends. He trusted me. You knew that I became a trustee of his estate, and I suppose this was a token of our friendship, and his gratitude."

"But why didn't you at least tell me?" Esther asked, still gazing at the picture.

"I didn't want to tell anybody. You must admit it's very unusual to be given a Picasso Blue. The real reason was that I was embarrassed to receive such a wonderful gift. I just kept it in the basement, hiding it even from the staff. I only looked at it in the evenings after the gallery had closed. There was also the problem of people making offers on it, if it became known in the market that Daniel Bromberg had a Blue Period painting in his gallery. No, it's best that nobody knows, Esther ... and now that you know, it must remain our secret."

His wife looked at him. Her initial anger at not being told began to disappear as she realised that at least now he was sharing his most valuable secret with her. "I hope you didn't keep it from me

16

because you were frightened I might tell one of my clients?!" she asked, smiling mischievously.

"No, of course not. If that were true, why would I show it to you now?" Daniel retorted defensively.

"I'm joking. I know you wouldn't think like that." She laughed, knowing that by merely suggesting it she caused her husband no small measure of discomfort. That was his punishment for not telling her everything.

# 6

Daniel hung the painting in their bedroom, away from prying eyes, preserving the secrecy about the painting and its whereabouts. Nobody would know that he had it, not even Lafarge's family, since the gift had been made in a private codicil. There were times when he and Esther would go into the room simply to look at the masterpiece. Despite its size, compared to the rest of his collection, which was an assortment of drawings, limited-edition lithographs and lesser oils, this painting stood out as a tour de force. Indeed it would have done so in any museum throughout the world. Daniel obviously knew this, and was equally aware of the painting's value. Insuring the work of art was no easy matter.

"Sometimes I wish that I could show it off to people." Daniel said quietly to Esther, sitting at the end of the bed.

"You mean, to let them know that you have it?"

"No, no not at all. I meant that it would be nice to

simply share the enjoyment."

"Well, there is no reason why you couldn't show a few friends. I am sure they wouldn't tell anyone if you asked them not to. It's only your paranoia about the art world, and the fear of any publicity, that keeps you from telling people."

"Oh, come on, Esther. You know as well as I do that once people know, I will have every dealer in Europe, let alone Paris, knocking at my door wanting to buy it." He paused. "Maybe, though, letting one person see it wouldn't hurt. It would be so satisfying to hear and see someone else's reaction. It would have to be somebody that I can trust implicitly."

"What about Roland?" Esther asked.

"Roland would be perfect. I'll ring him tomorrow."

# 7

Roland Bouget was Daniel Bromberg's oldest and closest friend. They met on the playground at kindergarten, where they had a fight over a football. The brawl lasted no longer than a minute before a teacher managed to pull them apart. The punishment they both received was a ruler struck against the palm of each of their hands. The pain they both experienced was so intense that it formed a bond between the two of them that had remained close until the present day. Roland had become an art critic for *Le Temps*, the forerunner of *Le Monde*, and was thus an ideal choice in every respect as someone with whom Daniel could share his secret.

The following afternoon he took Roland to his new apartment and led him into the bedroom.

"Hey, listen, Daniel, I know that we are close, but are you sure that this secret is something you want to share with me? And even if you are, I am not sure I want to go in there with you on my own!" Roland joked as Daniel opened the door.

"Oh, shut up, Roland, and just look."

"At what?" Roland looked around him, and then saw the crouched beggar with his bowl. He recognised immediately the greatness, and the majesty, of the work. He found it difficult to respond to his friend. He walked over to the bed, and sat down, speechless.

# 8

"So let me get this straight. No one knows you've got it, and I am not allowed to tell anyone. Why did you show it to me?" Roland asked, drinking his black coffee in the Bromberg kitchen.

"Because I trust you. You are the only person outside my immediate family that I can confide in. Also, I thought that you would appreciate it. You must promise me you'll keep it quiet."

"I will, but it's such a shame. I mean, despite its size it's probably the best Blue I have ever seen ... still, I suppose you have a point. Every client you have will want it, and in the end you probably would be forced to sell it notwithstanding what Lafarge said in the codicil."

"You see. I knew you would understand, Roland. Esther was right."

"Can I ask you an academic question?"

"Go ahead."

"Does anybody know that the painting exists? I mean, Lafarge was given the piece by Picasso himself as a gift for supporting him. We both know that the great man had no money at the time. If Lafarge didn't tell his family of its existence, and he left it to you in a separate codicil, there might be no record of the work."

"There probably is not. I know that none of the family knows about it. I am not sure that the artist would remember, but there is no point in me contacting him. I know that it's original, and besides which I want to keep my anonymity, especially with regard to this painting."

# 9

Daniel Bromberg's secret held firm over the following two years, as dark clouds descended over political Europe. As each Central European country fell under the influence, or indeed occupation, of the Nazi regime, Daniel began to make plans for himself and his family in the event of a war. However, it wasn't just the fascist threat which had worried the affluent art dealer during the last few years.

The worldwide economic depression that had ravaged places as far apart as the United States and Japan did not overlook Western Europe. France, herself, went through tremendous upheavals, with Paris experiencing some of the largest public demonstrations ever seen. It was not surprising that the economic malaise led to political radicalism, each movement hoping to provide answers to end the hardship. The fighting between the Communists, liberals and fascists steadily became worse, and faith in the parliamentary system began to be shaken.

"We are living in very uncertain times, Esther. Can you count the number of governments that we have had over the past five years. How can you be so sure that fascism won't take hold over here?"

"This is France, Daniel; it is not Germany. I am confident that Daladier will not fall. I also don't think the Germans will invade Poland. Certainly now that the British have given their guarantee as well as us."

"I can't believe that you are so confident. Do you think the people in Prague felt like that last year?"

"That was different. There were issues there with the Sudeten Germans. The Czechs were warned. Not only that, they provoked the Germans."

"I can't believe that you really think that. The whole thing was stage-managed by the Nazis. Esther, can you not see what is happening all around us? Can you not feel the menace threatening you?"

"Daniel, you are being overly dramatic. All I am saying is that I do not believe that we will have a fascist government here in France, and nor do I believe will we be invaded by Germany. The Nazis wouldn't dare. You seem to forget about our impregnable western front. Haven't you seen all

21

those films on the Maginot Line?"

"Oh, I've seen them. But I have also seen the films of the German Army in action. I don't think anything can stop them. And if you think that we are safe here you ought to think again. You might be right, and the fascists might not gain power here. After all, we had no reparation payments to make. But as far as a German invasion is concerned, I think there is a real threat."

"Daniel, they will not declare war on us."

"What happens if they invade Poland, and we are forced to declare war on them?" Daniel asked, walking towards her.

Esther sat still, unable to answer.

"Esther, what happens if the unthinkable happens and we have a swastika flying from the roof of the National Assembly? Have you thought of the implications? It might have escaped your imagination that we are Jewish, and no amount of assimilation will help us if we are conquered," Daniel whispered to her, crouching in front of her, in a similar pose to the beggar in the painting hanging above her head.

# 10

Daniel's words of fear and anxiety proved prophetic. As the German Army marched into Poland, both France and Britain declared war. Daniel had no illusions about his, and his family's, situation. Having wound down his gallery, he paid his landlord the outstanding rent. Under the circumstances he secured a good settlement.

Business had perversely been relatively good over the previous few years, and Daniel had managed to save enough money for his family to be secure. Ignoring the Bourse he kept all his money on deposit in the bank. He believed that the interest alone would be enough to see him through the dark tunnel that lay ahead of him. In this respect he could not have been more wrong.

The following May, 1940, the Nazis invaded France. Esther was right in that the Maginot Line would not be breached. But this was only because the Germans went around it, and swept down through northern France, destroying French resistance at Sedan. It was not long before Paris had surrendered and was under the subjugation of its new masters.

The Brombergs kept a low profile. Daniel tried to maintain some kind of normality, mainly for the sake of Marianna. The twelve-year-old daughter was not oblivious to the change in her surroundings. She constantly mimicked the goose step in the flat, but was sure to do it only in private or in front of her parents. She also noticed the change in her father's mood. From being gregarious and popular, Daniel had become withdrawn, sullen and introverted.

To break the melancholy pervading the apartment from suffocating them all, Marianna was intent on getting her father to join in with her games. One of these was racing up the eight flights of stairs which separated the fourth floor from the entrance hall lobby. The game had become a necessity in recent months since the lift had been out of order. For a twelve-year-old Marianna was physically relatively mature, and very athletic. As a result she possessed not only speed but also stamina.

At first Daniel was not at all enthusiastic but gradually through the love of his daughter, and in no small part to his improving fitness from the repeated climbs, he actually began to look forward to the '99-step challenge'. Despite losing every time, almost always on the last flight, the joy he received from seeing his daughter win was more than enough compensation.

"It's the last ten steps – I just can't do it! If only it was 89 and not 99 steps." Marianna smiled at her father sitting on the landing, panting heavily herself.

The mood in the apartment lifted, but only temporarily. Daniel soon returned to his depression as the German successes continued at an alarming pace. Esther tried to lift his spirits again, but it was no easy matter. He seemed resigned, only expecting the worst.

"Things are changing more quickly than ever before, and they are going to get worse. I heard this morning that in the East, in Poland, the SS are building ghettos. Warsaw, Lodz, Krakow and Lublin are the major ones. All of the Jews are being moved there. The conditions are terrible. Nobody knows what will happen next there, but I fear the worst."

"But it's not going to happen here. We are not put into ghettos like they are in Poland. They won't make us leave our homes. The people won't put up with it. Think of all our Gentile friends." Esther replied.

"Maybe you're right; maybe you're not. I can do no more than I have done. We'll just have to wait and see. The war situation looks bleak, and it won't get better unless the Americans come in." Daniel turned over, and switched out the light.

# 11

By the time the Americans did enter the War in December 1941, the Germans were in control of almost the whole of mainland Europe. The invasion of the Soviet Union, under the code name Operation Barbarossa, had started off with brilliant success for the Nazis. The only thing that could stop them was the oncoming winter. However, it was during that cruel winter that the German Army could see the red flag fluttering in the icy-cold wind above the golden domes of the Kremlin.

Life for the Bromberg family deteriorated rapidly over the following months, as the occupiers unleashed anti-Semitic measures on the French public. Everywhere the streets smelt of collaboration. Nobody knew whom to trust. One misplaced word could put someone in a concentration camp. However, it was Drancy that people in the capital most feared since it was so close to home.

The transit camp at Drancy, located not far outside Paris had originally been used to house refugees from the fascist regime in Spain. However, in 1940 these refugees were handed over to the Nazis and by 1941 Drancy became the main destination for French Jews who had been arrested by the French Police.

"I have managed to sell all of my remaining paintings. I didn't get anything like their true value for them. A mystery buyer suddenly appeared just when it seemed that nobody was interested. He obviously knew that I was desperate for the money. I don't blame him, I suppose," Daniel said quietly in a resigned manner to Roland, sitting on a bench in the Tuileries on an early summer's evening in 1942.

"What? All of them?" Roland enquired.

"I have kept one." Daniel took another drag from his Gitanes cigarette, and inhaled the smoke right down to what felt like the pit of his stomach. "I wouldn't sell that one. I don't know what I shall do with it when they come for me. And they will come for me. It's a matter of time." He was of course referring to the Picasso Blue.

"I can take it for you. I'll keep it for you until you come..." Roland stopped short.

"Would you? If I don't come back, or if none of us return, I want you to give it to a museum in Marianna's name. So people won't forget ... Sooner or later, the Allies will win this wretched war, and so many people will be forced to pay a price for their collaboration." He paused. "When can you come and pick it up?" Daniel asked anxiously "The sooner the better. I hear that there is going to be a series of raids, and that we will be shipped east ... to a concentration camp in Poland, or somewhere in the East."

"If I hear anything, I will let you know, Daniel. My contacts from the paper say that the Germans have built, or are still building, a number of these giant camps, where the Jews are taken ... and are exterminated. It defies belief, but the sources are reliable ones. The biggest centre is at a place called Auschwitz. Have you heard of it?" Roland asked.

Daniel nodded. His actions appeared as if taking place in slow motion. Even his speech had become deliberate.

"You know Roland, I can trust nobody ... only you. If they come for us, we probably won't be

coming back. I only hope they spare the children ...
Marianna. I mean, they couldn't possibly harm her,
could they?"

"I don't know, Daniel. There is no point in even
thinking about it. Besides, I haven't heard of any
imminent raids being planned, but if I do hear of
anything you will be the first to know. You could
leave for the countryside, and try and hide out
somewhere."

Daniel smiled at the suggestion. His friend did not
know that Esther was three months pregnant and
could hardly move. Her first pregnancy had been
difficult, but this one had made her very ill. She was
desperate not to lose it, despite the bleak future the
family faced.

"It's impossible. We'll take our chances here.
Maybe we'll get through it. Anyway, can you come
round tomorrow? I will have the painting ready for
you."

"I'll be there at six," Roland replied positively.

# 12

As Daniel walked away Roland noticed how frail his
old friend had become. Only in his early fifties, he
looked like an old man of seventy, hunched over,
with his jacket hanging loosely over his shoulders.
The pathetic sight unnerved Roland. He sighed, and
got up from the bench, and walked briskly to the
Hotel Crillon for his weekly appointment.

As he entered the hotel, he looked up and saw the

Nazi Swastika hanging still. There was not a breath of air on that humid night.

"Good evening, Monsieur Bouget. You are here to see Lieutenant Schleicher, I presume." The man at the doorway, dressed in the black SS uniform greeted his visitor as normal.

"Yes, that's right. I have some interesting information for him."

Roland was led to the elevator, and was taken to the fourth floor. Led down the narrow white-painted corridors of the famous hotel, which had become Nazi headquarters, Roland entered the office of Klaus Schleicher.

"Good evening, Klaus. How are you?"

"Yes, good, thank you, Roland. What is it that you want? I am very busy at the moment. Hauptsturm-führer Dannecker has arrived," the lowly ranked SS officer said abruptly, getting up from behind the desk and putting some papers away in a filing cabinet.

"Who's Dannecker?" Roland asked.

"What?! You don't know who Dannecker is?" He sat back at his desk, and shook his head in amazement. "Dannecker is the leading expert on Jewish affairs. He liaises directly with Eichmann in Berlin and with Oberg here. You do know who they are, don't you?" he asked sarcastically, referring respectively to the head of Jewish deportation and the leading SS officer in Paris.

"Yes, of course I do. But why is Dannecker in town?"

"The transport problems we had have now been sorted out. At last we can start sorting out the Jewish problem here in France. We have all the rolling stock necessary to deport not only the two hundred thousand Jews here in Paris, but also the five hundred thousand living outside the capital."

"Christ, Klaus, you are really going to do this? I mean, you will get resistance." Roland felt uncomfortable. As a collaborator, he felt little guilt. The financial benefits from the 'Aryanisation' of Jewish businesses outweighed any moral reservations he had had. But the deportation of hundreds of thousands of innocents did not sit so easily with him.

"What resistance, Roland? So many people have got their hands dirty already. Even we were surprised by the willingness of your people to collaborate. I don't think Pétain or Laval will have much problem with the Jews."

"Maybe you're right. I don't know. Is there anything else you want to tell me?" Roland asked.

"We are introducing the yellow star next week. All of the Jews will have to wear one, with the word *juif* clearly labelled in the middle." Klaus paused, looking Roland in the eye. "Now, Roland, you are not going soft on me, are you? You have been very useful to me so far. Don't let yourself down. We have made a lot of money together from your friend Bromberg's art. There will be others."

"Yes, well, *you* have." He paused, looking at the German's obvious annoyance at his retort. "No, of course I am not going soft. Actually, Bromberg is the reason why I wanted to see you."

# 13

"I am glad you told me this now, my friend." Klaus opened his desk draw and took out a box of cigars. He opened the box and offered one to Roland.

"Thank you." Roland unashamedly took the cigar.

"Are you sure of the provenance? I mean, is it definitely a Picasso Blue? There is no doubting its authenticity?" Klaus asked.

"There is no question that it is the real thing. But the beauty about all this is that nobody knows about it. Even the artist quite possibly wouldn't remember its existence. This time we won't have to pay off various middlemen to keep quiet, like the last time. We'll take it and hide it, and then sell it quietly. Nobody will know." Roland paused, taking a long drag of his cigar. "And this time, Klaus, we are talking of tens of thousands, not just hundreds of dollars."

"Yes, yes, I understand Roland. Now when are you picking it up?"

"Tomorrow at six."

"Good. Let me know when you have it in your hands. Do not tell anyone. This is just between the two of us. I will contact you."

Klaus showed Roland out of his office. He then closed the door and walked back to his desk, smiling to himself, not quite believing his luck.

# 14

The following morning Daniel Bromberg walked into his bedroom and removed the painting from the wall. He placed it carefully against the wall, using a cloth to protect it from marking. He then went across to the brown bureau and pulled open one of the drawers. There he found his black marker. Taking it, he went back towards the painting and knelt down beside it. He remained there thinking for some time, before turning the painting around leaving him looking at the blank inverse side of the canvas. He then carefully separated the picture from its frame. Instead of referencing the piece on the back of the frame as he would normally do, he felt around the rim at the top of the canvas, and unstitched the overlap. The extra piece of canvas was smooth and perfect for him to perform his task.

Lying down on his back, he began to write a number of characters on the underside of the material.

"What are you doing, Daddy?"

"Oh, nothing, sweetheart. Uncle Roland is borrowing the painting for a while, and I just wanted to check something." Daniel got up and carefully reattached the painting to its frame. The spare piece of canvas was then stitched back so that the code was hidden. Unless they already knew about it, nobody would think of unstitching it.

"Why?"

"Why, why, why! Honestly, Marianna, almost everything you say starts with a 'why'!" Daniel went over to his daughter, suddenly realising his sharp tone and unnecessary rebuke. "I'm sorry, darling. Uncle Roland is hiding the painting just in case the Germans take it from us. He is a good man, and wants to help."

Marianna nodded, and then placed her head on his shoulder. Daniel stroked her hair gently.

# 15

That evening at six o'clock precisely the door bell rang.

"Hi, Roland, come in." Daniel pressed the buzzer, and then opened the door and waited for his friend to come out of the lift.

As he ushered Roland into the flat, he looked carefully around the hall and the stairwell. Daniel was terribly anxious in case anyone should be watching.

"You can't be too careful, Roland. There are so many collaborators about. I wouldn't want you to get stopped for looking after my assets. You could face a stiff penalty if you got caught … Come on, I have the painting wrapped up for you."

Roland said nothing, but followed his friend through to the dining room, where the package was lying on the table.

"Are you OK?" Daniel asked.

"Yes, why? Do I not look well?" Roland responded, taking a cigarette packet out of his pocket.

"You are very quiet."

"Listen to me." Roland took his friend's arm. "The Germans are planning a massive round-up. Deportations are being stepped up. Nobody is safe. Yellow stars are being issued imminently. Every Jew will have to wear one. Daniel, you and your family are in real danger. Is there anything else you want me to keep for you?"

Daniel looked at his friend, shook his head and smiled. Totally unsuspecting, he picked up the package and gave it to Roland. "You are a good friend, Roland. I have heard lots of rumours about the round-ups, but so far they have all been proved to be groundless. However, I am not stupid enough not to realise that it is only a matter of time. As far as the yellow star is concerned, we have already been officially told."

"OK then, Daniel. Will I see you next week at the same time and place?"

"Of course. But you have to be careful now. People will be able to see that you are talking to a Jew. Don't put yourself into danger."

"Ach! I don't care what people think. I am your friend ... and always will be."

Roland hugged his old friend and left. As he left the flat, he smiled to himself, clutching the package tightly under his arm. He began to run down the stairs, and then out of the building and down the street. He then slowed down to a walk, barely concealing his excitement. The treachery and duplicity had been overtaken by the rewards of the prize. Trying to make sense of his actions, Roland convinced himself that he had given his friend enough warning about the deportations. It was more than most people were doing. Besides, it wasn't him who was guilty of promulgating these anti-Semitic policies. He was a victim of the war, too! He was simply making sure that he would get a share of his old friend's assets, rather than it all going to the Nazis. It was easy to find a way out of feeling guilty.

# 16

"So you have kept it safe. I would like to see it," Klaus said, standing up and facing the window, looking out over the Place de la Concorde.

"Don't worry, my friend. It is at my home. Nobody will find it. Nobody would look for it. Nobody knows that I have it ... That is, apart from you and Daniel, and I hardly think he will be looking for it!"

Klaus Schleicher looked at the figure sitting smugly on the other side of his desk. He had nothing but contempt for him. Although realising that collaborators were the lifeblood for SS operations in Paris, he could not help but despise them. They were all of a similar ilk: weak, cowardly, and lacking in moral fibre. They were the antithesis of what he imagined he himself was. Blood and honour was the order of the death watch, and he was intensely proud of his membership of the SS.

"You are right. Maybe I'll come round after the Jews have been deported." Schleicher walked back to the window.

"Have you a date for the first major round-up?" Roland asked, with a hint of enthusiasm.

"July 16th and 17th. We are going to transport about thirteen thousand of them out of Paris to the three detention camps at Drancy, Beaune-la-Rolande, and Pithiviers. From there they will be deported to Auschwitz," Schleicher responded, continuing to look out of the window.

"How are they going to be selected?"

"Oh, I don't know. I am not in charge, you know." The SS officer turned around and walked back to his desk, clearly beginning to lose his temper at these questions. "I am sure Eichmann or Dannecker will inform us of whom they want to get rid of." He stubbed his cigarette in the ashtray, and looked up. "Don't worry, Roland, the Brombergs will be included."

# 17

There was a spring in Roland Bouget's step as he walked back to his one-bedroom flat on the top floor of a building located on Rue de Chevreuse in the Montparnasse district. He sensed that deportation meant in effect liquidation. The Brombergs would never be seen again. The money from the sale of the painting would amount to many thousands of francs. He would not have to worry about his future financial security again. Schleicher had been totally honest when buying and selling the last lot of paintings, which came from Bromberg's private collection. It never entered his mind that he would behave differently over this one. Similarly, it never entered his mind how much he had changed over the last few weeks.

Before the Germans entered Paris, Roland had no political leanings towards fascism whatsoever. However, he came from a socio-economic group that proved to be a happy hunting ground for the Nazis. Of a lower-middle-class background, being the son of a butcher, he was desperate to succeed and make money. Neither success nor riches came quickly for him. Although he had managed to become an art critic at a major national newspaper, and had thus gained a certain status, this was nothing compared to the financial rewards that most of his friends had reaped prior to the invasion.

Resentment had become the order of the day. Everywhere he looked he saw others doing better. Now it was his turn. The propaganda released by the Vichy Government gave him an outlet to vent his hitherto hidden feelings. He began to think about what kind of people his friends were, and where they came from. Corrupting his thought pattern was the continual anti-Semitic bile that was published daily in the capital.

The idea of seizing an opportunity, and having the chance to succeed, arrived after a chance meeting with an SS officer in a cafe bar in the Rue de Rennes one sunny hot afternoon soon after the Germans had arrived in Paris. Roland was sitting alone outside when he was asked if the seat next to him was free. After nodding nervously, and recovering from an initial sense of discomfort at being seen in public with a Nazi, he began to warm to the officer's company. They chatted informally about a wide variety of topics, the most serious one involving the Jews, to which Roland provided a more than willing audience. The officer appeared to speak such sense that Roland was a convert to the cause well before the German had got up to leave.

"I must leave now, Roland, but it has been a pleasure to meet you. Here is my telephone number in the event that you want to contact me again. As I said, if you can be of any help, the rewards will be very great."

"Oh, uh, thank you ..."

"Please, you can call me Klaus."

"Fine. OK, Klaus ... I will be in touch."

Lieutenant Schleicher left the cafe and was driven away in his open-top black jeep. Roland stared at the piece of paper in his fingers. This was his opportunity. The anger and frustration began to have a meaning. He could help. He could be useful. His position in society was after all, as he now believed, due to the Jews. He began to believe that they were responsible for France's decline. He began to reflect on Blum's disastrous governments. He then thought about all of the rich people he knew, who seemed to be above economic recessions. He then centred on his old and best friend – Daniel Bromberg.

The idea of exploiting his friend's position obsessed Roland over the next few months. He managed to orchestrate the buying and selling of Bromberg's superb collection of Picasso watercolours, drawings and prints without the vendor knowing. He and his friend at the Hotel Crillon had unsurprisingly made a financial killing on the transaction.

As the sun had set on European civilisation, it was definitely rising on Roland Bouget. He had of course felt some guilt over what he was doing, but not enough to stop him. When he heard the

rumours about the death camps, which were being
built in the East in 1942, he did find himself in a
moral dilemma. But the lure of monochrome blue
helped him through any pangs of self-doubt. Roland
had now made his pact with the devil. There was no
turning back.

# 18

"That is what I have just said. Laval is insisting that
no French Jews will be deported at the present time.
It's put a bit of a spanner in the works," Klaus said
in a raised voice, clearly irritated by Roland's
repeated question.

"But ... but, then, who are being deported?"

"The lowest of the low. The refugees, or, as we
like to call them, 'stateless ones'. Laval has made one
concession to us. He's said we could include
children. Listen, it's a start." He paused. "Hey, don't
worry, Roland. I will find a way to make these
Brombergs disappear in the next big round-up!"
Schleicher smiled, his mood already changing for
the better.

"Are you sure? I was banking on them going. You
told me there was going to be a massive round-up
this week. Is that still the case?"

"Yes. The French Police are going to head the
operation, which is going to take place on the 16th."

"How many are going?"

"Thousands! But Vichy will have its way, and no
French Jew will be included, except, of course ..."

# 19

Under the code name Opération Vent Printanier, the French Police carried out the anticipated round-up of Jews. Known later as La Rafle du Vel' d'hiv, approximately thirteen thousand men, women and children were taken to the Vélodrome d'Hiver, a cycling stadium in Paris.

"Monsieur Bromberg?" the tall French policeman asked Daniel, after he had opened the door of his apartment.

"Yes. What do you want?" Daniel asked, knowing the answer already.

"Monsieur, you and your family are required to come with me at once. You have five minutes to collect together some necessary belongings. You are allowed to take with you underwear, shoes, socks, a towel, and a cup. Nothing else will be permissible. You have five minutes." He turned away and went back down the corridor.

Daniel closed the door gently, and walked back towards Marianna's bedroom. Esther was already in there waking up her adored daughter. Oblivious to the foreboding around her, Marianna got dressed in a daze. Not understanding why she was getting ready to go out so late in the evening, and being half asleep, she followed her mother's quiet orders to the letter.

Daniel had known about the impending round-up for days. He had his contacts, and was well-enough informed to know that wherever they were taken to, whether it be Drancy, Beaune-la-Rolande, or Pithiviers, their future was bleak. Deportation to the camps in the East was a near certainty. He had fully prepared Esther for the dreaded knock at the door. Now it had come, his wife appeared to be much more ready than he was. Like many Jews all over occupied Europe, being aware of the atrocities committed, had not resulted in him or his family fleeing the country. He had hoped that the heinous crimes being perpetrated by the Nazis were either untrue, or that the reports were massively exaggerated. He had also hoped that the dreaded knock would never actually come; but it had.

He quickly went to his bureau, took a piece of paper out of his drawer and wrote down with his black reference marker a cryptic message:

PBPbegà72AHM 99.4.10 pourM.MCMXLII

He stared at the code, knowing in his heart that if and when Marianna got it, she would be able to understand each and every aspect of it.

He folded the piece of paper and put it in his pocket. He then walked back towards his daughter's bedroom. Marianna had fully woken up now and was excited by the adventure which her mother had told her she was about to go on.

"Is everything ready now? You can only take…"

"I know. I heard him." Esther walked towards him, and embraced him tightly.

"Don't worry, my sweetheart. Things will be OK. Make sure that Marianna does not sense our anxiety," Daniel responded, giving the code to his wife.

"Are you ready, Marianna? Now, listen – you have to do everything the men in uniform ask of you. It is all part of the adventure."

"OK, papa, but where are we going?"

"You will see. Now come on."

The Brombergs shut the front door of their apartment for the last time. Walking quickly down the corridor, they then took the stairs down to the entrance lobby. They could hear the bus engine running, ready for their appearance.

"Ah, the Brombergs have finally arrived. Driver, this is the last family. You can go to the Velodrome now."

# 20

Daniel watched the policeman going through the list as the bus made its way to the Velodrome.

"Hey, Bromberg, what did you do?"

"What do you mean?"

"I mean, you must have really pissed someone off – you're the only Frenchman here!"

"What?"

The policeman got up and whispered in his ear. "Look around you. They're all Jewish refugees here. Tell me, what did you do?"

"Nothing. I promise. Absolutely nothing." Daniel turned around and looked at the people on the bus. "I thought they only cared about whether we were Jewish or not. Being French didn't come into the equation."

"That's where you're wrong. Laval put his foot down. Only refugees! Still, they obviously want you out. Your name has an asterisk next to it ... the Bosch have added you to the list."

"But that is ridiculous. I must speak to somebody."

"You'll have plenty of time at the Velodrome."

"Where?"

The policeman turned back to his seat at the front of the bus.

# 21

The victims arrived at the Velodrome late on the night of the sixteenth. They congregated in huddles all around the vast open-air stadium. The old and the sick were given no attention as the arena began to fill.

Daniel searched around, looking for help but more importantly for information. It was a fruitless exercise, as the Paris police refused to respond to any of his appeals. He slowly walked back to the area where Esther and Marianna were sitting.

"There is nothing we can do. I can only presume the worst, that we shall be transported to Drancy tomorrow."

"Why, Daniel? Why us? What have we done? Oh, God, why?" Have you told them that I am pregnant? Won't that help?" Esther asked desperately.

"No, I haven't, and it won't. The guards just don't care. Esther, I have no answers." He looked down at Marianna, who was sleeping in her mother's lap. "Have you put the note in a safe place?" he asked her.

"Yes. I managed to write down some instructions on the same note. Luckily, somebody smuggled in a pen! I've sewn it into the collar of her cardigan."

"Good. She'll be the last person they'll check for valuables or documents. If we come out of this hell, it will be important ... trust me."

# 22

The following morning Roland Bouget woke up later than usual, at around ten-thirty. He opened the window and threw open the shutters. It was raining. He leaned over the very small balcony, and stretched his neck around so that he could see all the way down the narrow street. It was unusually quiet. He walked back to his bedside table and took the half-smoked cigarette which was lying in the ashtray. He relit it and inhaled the unfiltered nicotine into what seemed like the pit of his stomach.

He looked around the small apartment. It had been, up until a few days ago, his only worthwhile possession. But now that he had the Blue, everything had changed. It was true that he had made money on the minor Picassos which Daniel had owned, but the lion's share of the profits had gone to Schleicher. He got down on his knees, his cigarette hanging out of his mouth, and looked underneath the bed. Stretching out his bitten-nailed hand, he grabbed the package. He carefully laid it out on the bed and unwrapped it. As he finally pulled the masterpiece away from the paper, he gazed at the image in awe. A tear welled up in his left eye. He felt an unfamiliar sense of superiority. He knew how to appreciate the work; he understood Picasso and his Blue paintings. He was an art critic. What did Schleicher know? How could he fully appreciate the magnificence of the painting?

Wild thoughts began to race through his mind. Should he make a run for it? He could easily buy a small cottage in the country, where he would be very difficult to find. He had enough money. Property was very cheap, particularly with cash.

Then, almost as suddenly as these fantasies had surged into his brain, resignation and fear pushed them back out. He would take the safer option.

# 23

With the crowding becoming more severe after the second night of raids, with over thirteen thousand Jews now held in the Velodrome, the situation was fast becoming intolerable for Daniel Bromberg. He walked around the stadium looking for anyone that he knew, without success. He wandered around, seeing babies and the very young, the elderly and the sick all exposed to this barbarism. His frustration grew at the lack of information, the lack of help, but most importantly at the lack of interest.

Every time he went back to his wife and daughter, his anguish increased. He could do nothing. Marianna, in common with many of the four thousand other children had developed diarrhoea. There being no toilets, the child was reduced to publicly humiliating herself. Esther tried as best she could to keep positive, encouraging Daniel not to despair, but it was a hopeless task.

# 24

Roland Bouget made his way to the Hotel Crillon. There was a spring in his step as he emerged out of the Metro and onto the Place de la Concorde. Feeling no guilt, and not bearing to think about the subhuman conditions his old friend was facing, he marched into the hotel entrance full of confidence.

"So it is in your apartment. Where abouts?" Schleicher asked.

"It's safe, don't worry."

Schleicher got up from behind his desk and walked over towards the window. Wearing the black uniform of the SS, Schleicher cut an impressive figure. The tunic fitted tightly over his upper torso. The black breeches were tucked into the highly polished boots. His back was towards Bouget, who could not see the anger in the officer's face.

He turned around and looked at the pathetic informer seated in front of him. He despised the sudden smugness of Bouget. He had been useful, but now that the Brombergs had been captured, and their art sold, his usefulness was almost at an end. There was only one thing left for him to do.

"Are you not interested in what happened to your friends?"

"No not all." Bouget squirmed. He really did not want to know.

"Well, I'll tell you anyway. They are all at the Vélodrome d'Hiver. They have been there for four days without shelter, with no food or health care. Already fifty of them have died. The children and the old are chronically sick with diarrhoea and God knows what ..."

"That's enough. I don't want to know any more. The whole thing is barbaric." Bouget got up to leave, desperate to avoid hearing more details.

"But I have not finished, and you do have to hear more. You have to hear it all, because you are part of this process. Tomorrow they will be taken from the stadium to one of the three transit camps outside Paris. Your friends will be going to Drancy. They will not be there for long. By the end of the week they will be in Poland ... and in a month..." Schleicher was now towering over the seated Bouget.

"Stop! Just stop! I have to go." Bouget got up. He suddenly felt a wave of nausea.

On leaving the SS Headquarters, Bouget made his way back to his apartment. He would leave Paris tonight. He had enough savings to buy a small cottage somewhere in the country, perhaps in the south, somewhere near Provence. There he would lie low until the war was over and things had settled down.

# 25

As soon as Bouget left his office the Obersturm-führer picked up the phone.

"Herr Müller?"

"Yes."

"It's Schleicher. I need you to do something for me."

"What is it?"

The phone call was brief and precise. Jurgen Müller was one of the many underpaid Gestapo thugs who were happy to moonlight on violence for extra money. The assignment he had been given was nothing out of the ordinary. However, the timing was a little unusual. He left the office immediately, and made his way to the Montparnasse district.

# 26

Roland Bouget was packing the last item of clothing into his suitcase when the buzzer rang. Stopping suddenly, because he was not expecting anyone, he walked cautiously over to the door.

"Who is it?"

"My name is Jurgen Müller. I have a delivery for you from a Lieutenant Schleicher."

As the Frenchman guardedly began to open the door, the German pushed it towards him with such a force that Bouget was knocked backwards onto the floor. Before he could get up Müller was on top of him, pulling him up and wrapping his right arm behind his back in a half nelson.

"Where is it?" Müller whispered in his captive's ear.

"What are you talking about?

"You know perfectly well what I am talking about. Now, tell me or I will break your arm." Müller slowly pushed his arm back to breaking point.

"Please stop. Please ... aaah!" Bouget screamed as he felt the unbearable pressure on his arm and shoulder.

"I haven't got time for this. Just tell me where it is and I will leave."

Bouget was in agony. Beads of sweat were dripping off his forehead as he tried desperately to work out his options.

"It's not here. I put it in a safe place."

Müller wrenched the arm up, and broke it, simultaneously dislocating the art critic's shoulder. Bouget screamed.

"Tell me where." Müller got up over the writhing body. He pulled out a pistol, screwed on the silencer, aimed it at the Frenchman's leg, and pulled the trigger. Another scream rang out. Müller then aimed at Bouget's crotch.

"No, no. Please don't. It's in the case on my bed. Underneath the clothing." The Frenchman could barely talk, almost losing consciousness from the agonising pain searing through his body.

Müller walked over to the bed and rummaged through the clothing. He found the smaller-than-expected brown package and pulled it clear. He walked back over to Bouget. Aiming his gun at the whimpering huddle on the floor, he fired the first shot into the Frenchman's groin. After a loud cry, he shot the second bullet into his head.

He bent over the body to make sure that there was absolutely no life left in it. Then he walked over to the window to see if there was any activity in the street. The screams had been loud, but these were unusual times for Paris: the unusual had become usual, the abnormal had appeared normal, and death was now part of everyday life. Seeing that there had been no reaction, Müller hurriedly messed up the flat. He wanted to make it look like a burglary that had gone wrong. Having broken a few lamps, thrown all the clothing on the floor, and cleared the books off the shelves, he left the flat and went directly to the Crillon.

# 27

On the morning of the fifth day, things had become desperate at the Velodrome. Marianna had become very weak. Daniel and Esther kept giving her water, not knowing if it was the water that was contaminated. They had decided to give their fourteen-year-old daughter their ration, too, on the basis that her level of dehydration was life-threatening. Esther had by now given up hope for her unborn child. At three months the pregnancy had been extremely difficult, and now with the lack of water and food the chances of going to full term were remote.

"My God, when will they let us out?" Esther

groaned to Daniel.

"It's hopeless. There is no information available. The police have become like the Gestapo." He paused. He rubbed his eyes and then sunk his unshaven face into his hands. "Esther, have you made sure that the code and your instructions are securely sewn into her cardigan?"

"Yes, don't worry." She looked down at Marianna, stroking her hair, and trying to shield her from the oppressive July sun. "You don't think we are going to make it, do you?"

"I don't know. It is hard to be rational in here." He looked around him at the squalid mass of people, strewn all over the Velodrome. Personal manners and hygiene had long gone. They had been replaced by basic survival. "If we get transported from here to one of the transit camps, our only hope is that we remain there. If we are sent from there to a concentration camp, then I am afraid that..."

Esther started to cry gently, rocking her daughter's head in her arms. She so wanted to see her grow up. The thought of her suffering was the greatest torture. She was such a happy girl, whose character was only starting to develop. How could they take away her life at such a young age? Why was God turning his back on them? She was not sure how much more she could endure.

50

# 28

That same day, the police entered the Velodrome and started rounding up the thirteen thousand Jews who had been left there for five days. With a brutality that none had experienced before, but most of whom would experience over the following few months with a frightening regularity, the wretched victims were herded into trucks.

Squashed together they made the short journey to the transit camp at Drancy. Still together, Daniel clutched the hand of Marianna. He glanced to his left and looked at his wife. He managed to free his right arm, and put it around her waist. He looked out of the small window and up into the fierce sunlight. He still had hope.

As the victims got off the trains, Daniel did not let go of his family. The situation rapidly descended into confusion, with hysteria and panic taking hold. The police tried to restore order, using their batons and their dogs. Slowly order was restored.

"Listen to me, everybody. All children under the age of sixteen please go to the left. Now!" the voice behind the megaphone shouted.

Daniel and Esther continued to hold on to Marianna. The thought of letting her go was too much for either to bear. The decision, within minutes, was taken away from them, as a French guard wrestled the fourteen-year-old free.

"Now, all adults who have no children must go to the left." The implication was immediately apparent and was not lost on Daniel. The enforced separation of parents from children was being carried out, cynically, in front of their noses.

The separation having been completed, new orders rang out, as Daniel and Esther were forced back on the trains.

"Don't worry, everybody. You will see your children very soon. There is nothing to be worried about." The faceless voice spoke calmly through the megaphone.

Most of the parents believed him. Daniel and Esther were not among them. During those two hours at Drancy, both of them knew that they would probably never see their beloved daughter again. At that moment Esther broke free of the guards and ran over to Marianna who was at the front of the long queue going into the camp.

"Marianna! Marianna!"

The little girl stopped.

"*Maman! Maman!*" She cried and ran towards her mother.

"Listen to me, my darling. Be brave. Daddy and I have always loved you. You will be fine. But you must promise me one thing. Look after this. Never lose it. Keep it at all costs," Esther said, pointing and tugging at Marianna's cardigan.

"But why?

"Eventually you will..." Esther was suddenly pulled away and thrown to the ground by a guard. Face down in the gravel, she was then kicked repeatedly, and bitten by the dogs which had been let loose on her.

Marianna was forced forward into the camp, but she was still a witness to the event. Daniel, who had watched the whole scene from the train, struggled to get off, but was held back.

"For God's sake, she's pregnant! Please..." he

screamed, whilst being restrained by the guards.

Having brutally assaulted her, one of the guards called off the dogs, and picked Esther up. Blood was seeping from the corner of her mouth. Hardly conscious but just managing to get up, she was pulled away by him and led to the side of one of the rail trucks. He propped her up against the wall. He put down his rifle and unbuttoned his trousers. He then pulled up her skirt, wrenched down her knickers, and placed his fingers forcefully into her, oblivious to her condition.

He then closed in on her, pushing his open mouth onto hers, trying to force his tongue inside her mouth. Esther, who was now fully conscious of the rape, tried desperately to push him away. She opened her mouth for air, but this merely gave her assailant the opportunity he had been waiting for, as she felt his tongue almost gag her. She was trapped and could not get away. Then suddenly she felt him force his way inside her. The pain of his intrusion was such that she screamed in agony. He did not relent, as he continued to violate her, driving his blood-gorged organ inside of her. He was now grunting heavily as his excitement increased. Esther was still trying to free herself, her legs kicking out, but it was to no avail. The guard was pushing harder and harder until finally he came inside her. He slumped over her body. She managed to push him off, but without his support she suddenly realised she had no strength in her legs, and collapsed.

The guard did up his trousers and rearmed himself. Picking her up, with a cruel smile on his face, he dragged her motionless body around to the front of the train and dumped her in the truck from where she had originally run.

"Esther, can you hear me?" Daniel whispered in her ear, not fully realising what had just happened.

There was no response.


# 29


Lieutenant Schleicher looked at the new acquisition in his luxurious third-floor apartment on the Avenue Foche.

"I don't know much about this sort of stuff. I mean, I am no expert. Obviously you can see that it is a masterpiece. What about you, Jurgen?"

"It all means nothing to me. How much is it worth?"

"Much more than you can possibly dream about," he mused. He looked up, suddenly realising that he was saying too much. "Oh, maybe not as much as I think! Why do you ask?"

"Relax, Lieutenant. We are friends. You have been generous with me," Müller said, holding up the brown envelope.

"I trust this will be the last I hear of this."

"Don't worry. Your secret is safe with me." He was about to go. "Oh by the way. The police found Bouget's body. They are treating it as a burglary. They'll round up the usual suspects. I have spoken to the relevant people. Everything is in order."

"Good, Jurgen, and thank you."

Müller left the apartment. Schleicher was still looking at the painting. He really couldn't appreciate the treasure. He didn't understand the magic and the beauty of the work. But he did understand its value. He placed the painting back in its wrappers and locked it away in his bedroom cupboard. He knew what he had to do. However, he did not expect to have to do it quite so suddenly.

# 30

The following morning Klaus Schleicher went to his office as usual. It was a beautiful late July morning. Stopping off for a coffee on the Champs-Elysées, he then picked up a newspaper and made his way to headquarters.

"Hans, why are there so many cars?" he asked the doorman as he entered the Crillon.

"The top brass are here."

"Oh! Like who?"

"Well, I know that Colonel Eichmann is here to see General Oberg."

"What? You mean *the* Eichmann. Adolf Eichmann from Berlin?"

"Yes, sir."

"Thank you, Hans. I'll be in my office." Schleicher marched on, wondering what all this was about.

Arriving on the fourth floor, he went straight to his office. His secretary was laying out his post on his desk.

"Where have you been?" She asked.

"I stopped for a coffee on the way in. Haven't I a quiet day today?"

"Well you did have until fifteen minutes ago. The General wants to see you immediately."

"Did he say what it was about?"

"No. He just wants you to see him."

"Well, ring him and tell him I'm coming up."

# 31

Schleicher walked past Commander Oberg's secretary, who immediately got up and ushered him into the office.

"Klaus, how are you? Thank you for coming up. Oh, relax no need for such formalities. Do you know Colonel Eichmann?"

"Only by reputation, sir. I am honoured to meet you," Schleicher said, relaxing his stance and shaking Eichmann's hand with a bow.

"Lieutenant, do you know the situation in the East?"

"Yes, sir. Well I know that the invasion into the Soviet state is going very well. I also know that my comrades are successfully making all conquered territory Jew-free."

"Yes, that is right. The *Einsatzgruppen* have been most successful, in very harsh conditions. As you know, it is completely necessary to rid ourselves of the Jew vermin. The very survival of the Reich depends on a pure Aryan race."

"Yes, sir," Schleicher replied, suddenly realising that his more-than-comfortable life was going to come to an end very soon.

"We have had to change our methods of getting rid of the Jews. What I am going to tell you is classified, and cannot be discussed anywhere else. Do you understand, Schleicher?"

"Yes, Colonel."

"In January this year a group of top-ranking officials met at Wannsee to discuss a solution to the Jewish problem. I arranged it. What was actually discussed there is not important to you, except to say that it was agreed that the extermination of the Jewish race is an achievable goal. Certainly in Europe. The method of extermination and where to exterminate them was also discussed." Eichmann walked over to the table and stubbed out his cigarette. He then continued.

"Oberführer Heydrich convened the meeting, and was officially put in charge, under the deputy Fuhrer himself, of what is now known as the Final Solution of the Jewish problem. As you know, unfortunately, our Oberführer was murdered earlier in the year in Prague. You are probably aware that we had our revenge."

"Yes. You mean Lidice." Schleicher was referring to the massacre of the male inhabitants of a Czech village.

"That's right. But we also of course accelerated our extermination programme under the newly named Operation Reinhard. Three massive camps have been built at Sobibor, Treblinka and Belzec. The last will be dismantled later in the year. It is estimated that as many as half a million Jews will be exterminated there alone. It is a magnificent achievement. The other two camps, plus Majdanek and Chelmno, and particularly Auschwitz are still very much operational."

Schleicher listened intently to the Colonel. Although he could not fully take in the numbers, he was clearly impressed.

"To keep to our targets, we need more manpower." The Colonel looked at the junior officer.

"I will do anything to help further the cause of the Reich." He meant what he said, having been overwhelmed with Eichmann's update.

"I know you will."

"Well, how can I help?"

"Auschwitz-Birkenau is the centre of the entire operation. Commander Hoess has introduced a new gas called Zyklon B, which has replaced carbon monoxide as the main instrument of death. It is far more efficient. We are now exterminating twelve thousand Jews a day at Birkenau. But to keep this rate up we need more officers. People who are skilled in organisation and efficiency. Men who can face this slaughter and rise above it, knowing that it is for the good of the Fatherland. Sometimes one has to do the most horrible acts for the common good of mankind ... There will obviously be a promotion for you."

"I understand, Colonel. I would be honoured to go there and help with the Final Solution."

"Good. Then it's settled. You will leave next month. Take two weeks leave before you depart. You will be fully briefed when you arrive. Good luck, Oberstürmfuhrer ... or should I say, Hauptstürmfuhrer!"

Schleicher got up immediately, stood to attention, and raised his right arm.

"Heil Hitler!" he shouted.

"Heil Hitler!" his two senior officers replied.

The newly promoted captain left the office.

"He is no relation to the old Chancellor?" Eichmann smiled, sipping his coffee.

"No, absolutely not. I've had him checked out. It is just a coincidence in the name. I mean, it's a fairly common name, isn't it?"

"Yes, of course. Well, as long as you are sure. I must admit, he does look promising, General. You were right – he will be just fine over there."

"I told you. Poor bastard! It's a hellhole. And working for Hoess! Ah well, I am sure he will do us proud." Oberg raised his coffee cup to Eichmann and laughed.

# 32

Schleicher went back to his office. He was both elated by the promotion, but also anxious about the prospect of going to Auschwitz. Of course he had heard about the camp, and the horrors that accompanied it, but he somehow knew that nothing would prepare him for what he was about to see. As soon as he got back to his desk, he started to look at his mail. He hurriedly took care of the outstanding administrative tasks, and then began to concentrate on the Picasso. He picked up the telephone receiver.

"Operator, can you get me Heidelberg 64380."

"Yes, sir. I will call you back."

The phone rang almost immediately. "Mother? It's Klaus."

"Hello, dear. How are you?"

"I'm fine, Mother. Listen, I'll be coming home next week for some leave. I need you to do something for me."

"Of course, just tell me."

# 33

The train left Drancy and went on to Pithiviers, where it stopped. Daniel managed to get out of the cattle truck, still holding his wife. He laid her out on the siding, and sat with her, waiting for the next set of orders to be barked at him. He sat back against the concrete wall, hardly managing to keep his eyes open. He stroked his wife's hair. He then began to think of Marianna, and how she was coping with the desperate task of survival. He looked across at Esther. Her dress was torn. There was blood all over her legs, the legacy of her unborn foetus. She seemed lifeless. He gently held her arm and whispered in her ear, trying to wake her, but to no avail.

The victims remained at Pithiviers overnight. Without food or water, they were also denied basic hygiene necessities. Forced to urinate and defecate in the open in front of everybody reduced them to the status of animals. This was no sudden barbaric decision, but part of a systematic program developed by the Nazis to treat their victims as subhuman.

The following morning they were given water and pushed back into the cattle trucks. This time the trip would be far longer. Hundreds of them were squashed into each truck, barely having enough room to breathe. Daniel carried Esther towards the train, but was stopped by the guard.

"Wait. Leave her here."

"I would rather take her with me. She'll be fine soon." Daniel looked at her.

"I said 'leave her'!"

"No," he replied.

Daniel then felt a searing pain at the back of his head as the guard hit him with his baton. He fell down on top of Esther. Half-conscious, he was pulled away by the guards and forced into the trucks. He tried to fight back but was unable to do so.

The train pulled out, beginning its eastward journey to Poland. The guards picked up the body of the dead woman lying near the train, and threw it down with the other dead victims piled on the siding.

# 34

The journey lasted three days and nights. Under the most awful conditions, the passengers, perhaps better described as cargo, experienced the worst conditions that they had ever had to endure. In the baking heat of summer, with very little water, and hardly any fresh air, the victims had to stand for the entire journey; there was no space to fall. The train stopped and started on numerous occasions, making the transit even more unbearable.

Finally, the train entered the valley of the shadow of death. Slowing down to almost crawling speed, spewing out its steam almost continuously, it stopped close to the watchtowers that overlooked the platform at Auschwitz-Birkenau. The infamous spur, which later took the trains to the very entrance of the death camp, had not yet been constructed. The train came to a halt. Moments later the truck doors were unlocked and slung open. What confronted the prisoners was a vast complex of long huts stretching out into the distance. As they disembarked onto the platform, the guards and their dogs harassed them, both continually barking at them. The cacophony of shouting and screaming was deafening, leaving the sorry victims completely bewildered.

As they looked right they could see the main watchtower, and in the far distance the massive network of barbed wire and perimeter fencing. But it was to the left where the main construction facilities were located.

Daniel looked at the two major concrete blocks approximately a mile away, both of which had enormous chimneys towering into the sky. Smoke was billowing continuously. The stench was unbearable. Daniel had never experienced an atmosphere like this. The noxious aroma of burning flesh was everywhere. Having been marched towards the camp, he now stared at the plain brown buildings where people were already being told to go to for registration and showering.

He now had no doubts what all this was about. He had his contacts in Paris and had been told in the last few weeks of the construction of new death camps. He did not want to believe them. But these were the gas chambers and crematoria he had heard about. He now had no illusions about what was going to happen. But he had had enough. Esther was gone. In all probability, Marianna, if not already dead, would be so in a matter of weeks. What was there for him to live for? He certainly had no desire to stay in what was akin to Dante's Inferno.

Having noticed the long queue into the buildings, and the lack of any people coming out, Daniel had put two and two together and realised that this was the assembly line of death. The selection process for the gas chambers was taking place in front of him. The fitter were told to go to one side, while the sick, the very young, and the elderly were told immediately to join the queue to the 'showers'.

"You! Go over there." The guard shouted at him, forcing the butt of his rifle into his ribs.

Daniel doubled up in pain and fell to the floor.

"Get up. Come on, get up. There is no time."

Daniel tried to lever himself up, but still very weak from the lack of food and water, and totally exhausted from the journey, he could hardly move.

"He's no good. Send him over there." The guard told two camp prisoners to take Daniel to the 'assembly line'.

Suddenly the instinct for life gripped Daniel. He didn't want to die. With all his strength he pushed himself up. But it was too late. He was forced to join the line.

# 35

Stripped of his clothing, his hair having been shaved off, he was pushed into a large room, ostensibly for his shower. He was one of hundreds crammed into the space. He looked up at the ceiling and saw that there were no shower heads. He then looked around him. Some people were excited just to be off the trains and with the expectation of having some water on their bodies. Others were simply quiet not showing any emotion. There were some who were petrified and who were screaming.

The doors were slammed shut and darkness enveloped the victims. Suddenly, almost instantaneously everybody realised that this was no shower room. Fear engulfed the entire mass of naked men as they tried to move. Kaddish was heard as hundreds of the men began to recite out loud the Jewish memorial prayer.

The sound of crystals being deposited on the grates above them was heard. Then as the Zyklon B mixed with the air, it dissolved, releasing a lethal gas which began to suffocate the victims. Sometimes it would take over half an hour for all of them to die. Daniel began to feel nauseous and started to lose consciousness.

# 36

Klaus Schleicher looked out of the train window and saw in the distance his home town. He looked up at the old castle on the mountain. He had spent his entire childhood here in the old university town of Heidelberg. He reminisced about all the wonderful times he had had here with his family. Everything was so peaceful.

The train reached the station. He looked out of the window and saw his mother waiting for him on the platform.

"Klaus!" she shouted, walking over to the compartment door.

"Mother! How are you?"

"I'm fine. How long are you here for?"

"Two weeks," he replied, hugging her.

"Then where are they sending you?" A worried look overtook her face.

"Come! Let's get in the car and go home. We'll discuss it later. They have just promoted me. I am now a captain in the SS!" He put his arm around her and walked towards the car-parking area.

# 37

Helga Schleicher was a decent woman. Blonde and blue-eyed, she was a classic example of what every

Nazi dreamt of as a perfect Aryan. Still only forty four years old, she had lost her husband twenty-six years earlier at the battle of Verdun. She was pregnant with Klaus when she received the devastating news. She hadn't remarried, although she did have a number of admirers. She was still extremely attractive.

Coming from a relatively prosperous middle-class family, Helga managed quite comfortably in bringing up her son. She was totally devoted to him. His education was paramount to her, and she spared no expense in paying the best tutors to help improve Klaus's academic standards. The devotion paid off when he won a place to read law at the University of Heidelberg.

It was at university that Klaus became attracted to the Nazi cause. He became a party member and was recruited by the SS. His belief in Hitler, the Fatherland and its destiny of hegemony over Europe was sincere. He had no problem with the vicious anti-Semitism which was the core of the party's ideology.

He qualified as a lawyer with the minimum amount of work. Ironically it was the party that encouraged him to finish his studies. It needed young professionals in the mainstream, to help it in its vast legal and constitutional programme. People like Klaus Schleicher were extremely valuable. However, Klaus was not interested in the law at all. He just wanted to get involved in the party, and take part in the historic fight for German Aryan superiority. He immediately won a commission and saw service first in Czechoslovakia, and then in Poland, where he was stationed in Krakow. Here he was mainly involved in the setting up of the ghetto, that would accommodate the large Jewish population. His organisational skills attracted the attention of his superiors, who transferred him to Paris to help in setting up the legal framework for the future Aryanisation of France.

This had been his main work over the past fifteen months. Approaching his twenty sixth birthday, he was now ready for the East. He was looking forward to being on the front line dealing with the eternal enemy of the Reich.

The one sour note to his career development was the reaction of his mother. Horrified at the rise of Hitler, and the radicalisation of the Nazi Party, she was one of millions of silent objectors. She hated her son being involved with the uncontrolled violence. She also hated the unprovoked attacks on the Jews, some of whom were personal friends. By the time the war started, her relationship with her son had severely deteriorated. She was still devoted to him, despite her obvious disapproval, but he had distanced himself from her. His devotion was to the party. There was no room for anybody else.

The telephone calls at first were frequent and regular. But by the time he got to Paris he hardly rang at all. He could not understand his mother's antipathy to the party; her lack of respect for the people he was mixing with; and her lack of interest in his career. All she was interested in was whether he would be going to the Eastern Front. That was her biggest fear. She knew that if he went east she would probably never see him again. Her hope was that he stayed in Paris until the war was over.

# 38

"Well, did you open the safety-deposit box account at the bank?" he asked as she turned the engine on.

"Of course. Herr Schmidt was most accommodating ... Klaus, what is all this about?"

"When can we see him?" he replied, ignoring her question.

"Whenever! He's expecting you. Klaus, please tell me – where are you being sent, and what is all this about?" Helga was clearly anxious.

"Well, you might as well know now ... I'm going to the East."

"Oh, my God. I knew it. When?"

"No, Mother, don't worry – it's not the front. I have to work behind the lines helping with the resettlement programme."

"What resettlement? ... You mean the Jews."

"Yes. The camps – I mean the settlements – are in Poland, and nowhere near the front. You should be happy for me. It's perfectly safe, and I won a promotion."

"Happy!" She laughed sarcastically. "Happy that my son is going to a labour camp in the East; that he is a racist; that he is throwing his life away for a barbaric cause; happy that his idol is a madman. Happy that..."

"That's enough! I will not have you talk about the Führer in that way. I will also not allow you to say such things about the cause. It amounts to treason. Perhaps it is better in future that you don't know where I am going or what I am doing."

"Perhaps you are right."

"Good. That's settled. I do not want to talk about it again. I want the next two weeks to relax, without any arguments. Do you think you can manage that?"

"Yes, Klaus. I can manage it. Shall we go to the bank now, rather than go home?"

"Why not."

Helga Schleicher took a sharp left turn and drove towards the bank where Herr Schmidt would be expecting them. She glanced across at her son, who was staring out of the front windscreen. She thought back to his youth and what a wonderful child he had been. Obedient and kind, he had been a model son until the party had got hold of him. He had since become as bad as the rest of them. A cold shiver ran down the back of her neck with the realisation that at that moment she stopped loving him. Worse still, she resented him being a part of her life. Everything she believed in, and stood for, was an anathema to him. He represented evil, and nothing would change him. She had even lost interest in why they were going to the bank at all.

# 39

"Herr Schmidt, it's good of you to see my son and me."

"It's not a problem, Frau Schleicher. It is both a pleasure and an honour to be of service," the bank manager responded, deliberately in that order, looking admiringly straight into the eyes of his friend and client.

"Herr Schmidt, is there somewhere we can talk?"

The bank manager managed to avert his gaze and looked across at the SS officer. His attitude immediately changed.

"Yes, of course. Come this way." He ushered the pair into his private office, clearly ill at ease with the black-uniformed officer.

"I do hope that there is nothing wrong. I am a party member!" He shakily took out his wallet and showed his card to Klaus. The genial bank manager was very nervous. Although he indeed was a member of the Nazi Party, he was not at all active in politics. His employers had insisted that he became a member, and for the sake of his career he had joined up.

"Why should there be anything wrong, Herr Schmidt? It is me who asked to see you, through my mother. I am sure you are loyal to the values of the Reich."

"Absolutely! Of course ... Now, what would you like?" He looked across nervously at his friend Helga.

Schleicher opened his case and carefully took out the painting, which was still wrapped in brown paper. Careful not to unwrap it, he placed the package on the desk.

"I would like you to keep this for me. It is a very valuable painting which was given to me by an old friend. I would rather not tell you what it is. But suffice to say that it is by a very well-known artist. In the event I do not return from the war, the painting will belong to my mother."

"That is fine. There is no problem. Do you have any proof that it is yours? I mean, what if somebody else claims it later, in the event that you do not return."

"May I remind you, Herr Schmidt, that you are talking to an officer of the Reich. I can also guarantee you that nobody else will claim possession or ownership of it."

Helga Schleicher squirmed in her chair. One did not have to be too clever to work out where the painting came from. She said nothing.

"Of course, Captain Schleicher. Your instructions will be followed to the letter. It will be kept here in safe custody. You can rely on my complete discretion in this matter." He took out a form from his desk. "Please sign here, and here. Thank you," the bank manager said in a curt tone.

"No, thank you, Herr Schmidt." Schleicher returned the pen.

The three of them got up and went straight to the vault. Schmidt took it to the oversized deposit box. He gave the key to the officer, who in turn passed it to his mother. Deposited in box number 88, appropriately numbered, the painting would remain there for the rest of the war.

"Maybe we might go out one evening, Frau Schleicher?" Schmidt asked as mother and son got into the car.

"I think not, Herr Schmidt. My mother will be very busy over the next few weeks. Goodbye," Schleicher responded, driving off.

His mother reprimanded him. "I am fully capable of responding on my behalf, thank you."

"I wouldn't want you to see him. He's a lackey. You can do better than that."

Franz Schmidt had been a good friend to Helga. He had been kind to her during the interwar years, helping her settle her late husband's estate. Although her son did not know it, Helga had seen the bank manager on a number of occasions, and had struck up a close relationship. Although short in stature, and slightly obsequious, he was still a relatively decent man who provided her with more than a small amount of support.

In contrast to the gratitude she felt towards Schmidt, her revulsion at her own son was growing daily. She had no wish to keep the painting if it was left to her. She would make that clear to the custodian when she saw him. There was no doubt that the painting had been stolen. Her son's guarantee had meant that the poor owner had been killed. She was now sure that the monster she had created was capable of killing somebody.

# 40

Marianna and hundreds of other children spent the next four weeks at Drancy. Like the rest of them she was extremely frightened. At fourteen years old, she was certainly not the youngest child there, but nor was she the oldest. During the first week she constantly thought about her parents and when she was going to see them again. She hoped her mother was all right now, having seen her beaten by the guards on the platform.

Despite the foul rotten smell of wet straw she managed to sleep. She got used to the noise at night: of the dogs barking, the guards shouting, the children crying, and the sporadic shooting. The pathetically small rations of soup and bread kept her alive. She talked to no one. She wandered around the camp, hiding in the various recesses of the U-shaped multi-storey complex, which had been the old police barracks before the war.

By the third week she had become so preoccupied with survival that she stopped thinking about her parents, and just concentrated on getting through each day as it came. The barbarity around her hardened her instincts for survival. Although only fourteen, those first weeks in captivity matured her well beyond her years. She knew that they would all be leaving soon, but she had no idea of when and where.

During the fourth week some of the other children began to follow her around. By default she became a leader. Since the name of the game was survival of the fittest, there was no doubt that Marianna Bromberg was a very strong girl who had adapted better than most to the inhumane conditions. She kept the younger ones' hopes up by telling stories; the older ones were encouraged to forage for food, and to find new hiding places. Above all, in Marianna's little gang, which numbered twelve children, there was a prohibition on crying. Nobody was allowed to cry, except when in bed and where no one could hear or see them.

When the inevitable roll-call happened at the end of the fourth week, Marianna had changed from a protected little girl, racked with stomach cramps and diarrhoea into a strong adolescent who had adapted to her environment and was ready to fight for her survival at whatever the price.

# 41

"Bromberg!" The voice shouted.

Marianna stepped forward and joined the queue of children who were going to leave the camp for 'resettlement'. Of her small gang, only two were left behind. There was no apparent reason for this. Nothing was explained. What was certain was that they too would be transported eventually.

The children made their way to Bobigny train station, where the railroad cars were waiting to take them to Auschwitz.

"*Raus! Raus! Vite ... Dépêchez-vous!*" The German guards and French police on the platform shouted at the children, pushing them into the trucks. There was no time to be wasted. The Nazi genocide programme had a timetable that had to be kept to. All other wartime operations would be relegated in importance. The trains had to run on time. The extermination of the Jews was paramount. From Drancy alone, over sixty thousand Jews were deported to Auschwitz between 1942 and 1944.

Just as her father had been a month earlier, Marianna was squashed into the car. With her mindset now trained on survival, she managed to push her way to the back where there was a small vent. From this opening she would get all the air she needed to survive the suffocating heat.

# 42

The two weeks Klaus Schleicher spent with his mother were peaceful and uneventful. Having secured his financial future with the deposit of the painting, he relaxed. He hardly talked to his mother. If anything, their relationship disintegrated even further. Very little was said, as Klaus sunbathed in the garden and read. He never told his mother about Auschwitz specifically, or what he would be doing there. She wouldn't understand that it was an honour for him to be part of the Reich's most important mission. Not only that, he felt he could not trust her. She had displayed all the traits of bourgeois weakness, especially regarding the Jews. Sympathy was something he would not tolerate.

"Mother, I will be leaving very early tomorrow. I will not be back for some time. There is an enormous amount of work to do out there."

"I understand, Klaus." A tear slipped out of the corner of her left eye. She was still his mother and however hard she tried she could never cut him off completely.

"It will be difficult. You see, it's hard for me to explain what a fantastic opportunity it will be for me out there. You just don't understand."

"No. I don't. Perhaps I never will. In a way I don't want to know where you are going or what you are doing. It revolts me to hear about the atrocities that are being committed. Biologically, I have to love you because you are my son. It's a necessity. But as a human being, Klaus ... Please, please tell me you won't be involved."

He got up and walked out of the room. He would not lie to her, so it was best to ignore the question. He went directly upstairs to pack. Disgusted by his mother's attitude, he could not bear to be with her any more. One more evening, and then he would be gone. What he hadn't realised was that his antipathy towards his mother was more than matched by her disgust for him.

# 43

The private plane, a Junker 88 laid on for him by SS headquarters, left Heidelberg the following morning at six. The flight would take just under three hours to cover the five-hundred-mile journey to Krakow. As the plane took off, he was filled with a sense of anticipation. At last he was going to be part of the real war. Yes, he had left the comforts of the desk job at the Crillon. But now he felt he was going to be doing something really useful. He was going to be part of the destiny of the Third Reich.

# PART THREE

London: September 1995

The Royal Academy

# 1

She had been looking forward to the exhibition for a number of months, but now the opening had finally arrived. Marianna Bromberg had always loved twentieth-century art, and the Picasso Retrospective, which had toured the world to much acclaim, offered a unique chance to see all the major paintings in her home city in one visit. The alarm woke her up at eight; she had showered and was dressed by eight-thirty. When the door-bell rang fifteen minutes later, she executed the near impossible task of pressing the intercom and telling the driver to wait, whilst holding a mug of coffee in one hand and a slice of toast in the other.

Clutching her handbag, and snatching the ticket from the mantlepiece, she left her flat in Kensington Court. In the lift she glanced at the ticket, which clearly showed an opening time of ten o'clock. She had calculated that the taxi would take fifteen minutes at this time in the morning. The queue would not be too long.

"There's been a lot of interest in this exhibition. It was mobbed there last night," The taxi driver remarked.

"Was it? God, I hope the queues aren't too bad. This morning is the first day for the public,." She replied.

"No, I think you'll be all right. I just passed there, and there were very few people waiting," He reassured her.

As the taxi drove up Piccadilly, Marianna saw the back of the line, at least two hundred yards long.

She sighed as she saw the queue. She then smiled at the irony of the situation. She had stood in lines before, and had experienced far longer waits.

2

She entered the gallery at ten-thirty. Walking up the giant staircase she entered the exhibition area, which was laid out in the chronological order of his works. She walked slowly around each room, cross-checking every piece with the exhibition guide to make sure she had not missed anything. Generally she knew more than the flimsy pamphlet offered, but she nevertheless clutched it as a reference note. Having spent forty-five minutes in the first room, and being fully satisfied that there was really nothing else to see, she walked into Room Two.

Surrounded by the most beautiful blue and rose-coloured paintings, Marianna continued her tour. Suddenly, out of the corner of her left eye, something made her hesitate. She tried to concentrate on the painting in front of her. The magnificent *Family of Saltimbanques* was arguably the finest painting of his Rose Period. A giant seven-by-seven-foot painting of five itinerant acrobats and a solitary woman, it was a masterpiece in the truest sense of the word. Reflecting the sadness and the poverty of the artist, it is regarded as one of Picasso's finest works. But at that moment Marianna could have been looking at the *Mona Lisa*, and it would have made absolutely no difference.

It was not as if she did not know what she was looking at. She was fully aware of the painting in front of her. She knew what to look for and what to appreciate. But the distraction made the whole exercise useless, indeed pointless. She gave in. Turning her head slightly to the left, she looked at the small blue painting placed incongruously next to the giant pink. She suddenly felt weak. Her heart began to race, and her face began to feel hot and flushed. She walked towards the painting and stopped directly in front of it. Very few people had taken much notice of it. The hang had been ill-conceived, given the disproportionate sizes of the paintings next to each other. It was almost as if they were trying to hide this particular blue painting of a young beggar crouching with his bowl.

Marianna stared at the image, which was so familiar. She felt very faint, but managed to rise above her physical weakness. She stood fixed to the spot. Memories started to flood her mind. Memories she had left in the wilderness since she was liberated from Belsen Concentration Camp in April 1945 were suddenly reacquainting themselves.

A tear welled up in her left eye, and fell slowly down her cheek. She suddenly felt overwhelmed by a kaleidoscope of emotions. She wavered and then fell, immediately losing consciousness.

# 3

"Are you all right madam?"

"Yes, yes, I'm fine."

"Now, take it easy, and get up slowly. You've just fainted!" The guard tried to help Marianna to her feet.

"Oh, thank you. You are kind. I'm so sorry. This hasn't happened before," she said, rather embarrassed at seeing all of the people looking at her.

"OK, everybody. This show is over. Please carry on with what you were doing!" the guard shouted to the onlookers.

"Now, you come with me to the Friends' Room, and get some tea inside you."

"Thank you. But will it be possible to come back in?"

"Don' be so soft, madam. Of course you can." He smiled and took her to the private members' lounge.

Marianna relaxed in the quiet surroundings of the Royal Academy's Friends' Room. She was back in control of herself. It had been a long time since she had let in those memories. She knew now that she would have to confront them. Her pre-war recollections had always been vague. The horrors of Auschwitz and Belsen were clear in her mind. She could never forget what she suffered and endured there. But, prior to that, her childhood in Paris was so distant. It was like a dream. The crouching blue beggar had rudely reawakened her.

# 4

By the time she had finished her cup of tea, Marianna was ready to return to the gallery. She still felt confused. The vague memories of the painting were dancing around in her mind. She remembered her father hanging it up; her mother's reaction to it when she first saw it; and seeing her father's face when he gave it to Uncle Roland on that midsummer's evening: these thoughts were suddenly invading her brain as she entered Room Two of the exhibition for the second time. And what did happen to Uncle Roland?

She walked slowly towards the painting. It was beautiful. She then read the description of the work in the pamphlet. Looking up once more, but this time looking at the brief provenance next to the painting itself, she read the details:

'*The Crouching Young Beggar with his Bowl*

On loan from the Schmidt family'

Marianna took her pen out of her bag, and wrote down the details on the exhibition guide. Ironically, since she had been looking forward to the exhibition for such a long time, she no longer felt interested in seeing the rest of the paintings; she left immediately to go home.

# 5

Although only sixty-seven years of age, Marianna Bromberg looked much older. The war years had taken their toll. More than two years in Auschwitz, and then six months at Bergen-Belsen, stole away her youth. The typhus she suffered after liberation took another six months away. Full health returned in her late teens, and by then she looked like a woman. Everything else followed suit. Physically she always seemed old beyond her years, but mentally she was always razor-sharp.

Having arrived at her flat, she knew immediately what she had to do. "Hello, is that the RA?"

"Yes it is, madam. How can we help?"

"Can I speak to somebody who is involved with the current show? The Picasso show, that is."

"Yes, certainly, madam. Please hold." There was a long wait, then, "Hello?"

"Yes. I was looking through the catalogue of your current Picasso exhibition."

"Yes?"

"And I was wondering if one could contact any of the owners who had loaned their pictures?" It was a speculative question to say the least.

"Well, most of the pictures have been loaned by various art galleries. There are very few still privately owned."

"It was the small blue painting of The Crouching Young Beggar with his Bowl I was particularly interested in. You see, I am doing a thesis for my university degree on this particular period of Picasso, and I would very much like to find out more about this painting."

"You sound quite old to be a student."

"I am a mature student," Marianna quickly responded.

"Let me look then. Yes, a Herr Schmidt gave that piece to the exhibition. I really can't tell you any more."

"Oh! That's a shame." Marianna paused for what seemed like an eternity, trying by her silence to coax some more information out of the exhibition assistant.

"Well, I could tell you the dealer's name and address, I suppose ... Yes, here it is. The Breitner Gallery in Heidelberg. The name of the dealer is Gustav Breitner. I am sure he will be able to help you with your enquiries."

# 6

"Are you sure you want to go through with this? It's been a long time Marianna." The young French doctor asked her.

"Oh, Candice, I don't know. You are right in that it has been a long time. But since I saw it again, I feel I have to do something. I had blocked out of my mind all of my pre-war childhood. I'd almost forgotten my parents. Their smell, their touch, even the way they looked. But seeing that young beggar made me remember them again. It made me think about them, and it's almost as if I owe it to their memory to get that painting back. I know I don't need it! But I remember how much my father loved it, and how much he would have wanted me to have it."

"Do you have anything, and I mean anything, to prove that it was ever yours?"

"Just the memory of it hanging in our flat ... And of course Uncle Roland keeping it for us!"

"Who was he?" Candice asked fascinated.

"He was my father's best friend. He was an art critic for *Le Temps*. I don't know why I remember that but I was so impressed at the time that someone I knew had their name in the paper! I remember him taking the painting for safe keeping. And that is it."

"Why don't you start with him then? The Schmidt family in Heidelberg will have to wait."

"I can't go back to Paris. You know that, Candice. I couldn't bear that."

"If you want your painting back, you're going to have to go there. You need more proof."

# 7

Marianna flew to Paris the following week. She was not looking forward to going back to her old home. She had avoided returning to the city as much as possible. The last time she had been back was fifteen years ago when her Aunt Beatrice died. As the plane landed at Charles de Gaulle, her heart began to pound against her chest cavity. She managed, however, to keep things under control. She knew what she had to do. There was nothing emotionally difficult about her task. Having sent a very long letter explaining exactly what she was looking for to the documents department at the Georges Pompidou Centre, she was given a time to look up the information she needed. Arriving at Châtelet-Les Halles, she was taken to the building where the microfiche records were kept. Everything that she had asked for was waiting for her. She took off her coat and sat down at the desk where the relevant records had been placed. She carefully looked at the first fiche.

'*Le Temps* journalist murdered.' The headline stared at her. She glanced at the date, which read July 21st 1942. She then read the article.

'Roland Bouget was murdered last night at home. Bouget was a junior art critic for *Le Temps*, and was highly regarded by his colleagues. It appears he was a victim of a burglary that went wrong. He was brutally assaulted and shot dead from a close range. Police are searching for clues. At present they have no suspects.'

She sat back in her chair, astonished at poor Uncle Roland's terrible fate. It was a terrible coincidence that he had been murdered at the same time as, she presumed, her parents were killed.

She took the microfiche from the magnified glass lamp, and then saw the other fiche on her left. Assuming that this would simply be a follow-up, on the previous article, telling her that the police had found the murderer, she quickly placed the fiche under the lamp. If the first article had surprised her, she had no idea of what was about to hit her in the next one.

'War Trials Reveal More Collaborators', ran the headline. 'Roland Bouget, it was revealed today in a court room in Lyon, has been exposed as one of the Nazis' most important collaborators. During the trial of Jurgen Müller, a Gestapo police officer, it was heard that Bouget, an employee of *Le Temps*, regularly supplied the SS in Paris with information, particularly relating to the Jews. He was murdered four days after the Great Raid of the Vel d'hiv, in July 1942.

'It was later claimed, during the prosecution's summing-up, that Müller had killed Bouget in his flat. He was trying to recover a piece of art for the SS. Müller has admitted his guilt in the murder. It has not been established who gave the orders for the murder, or where the painting went. Müller could not remember the details of the painting. Müller was sentenced to ten years in prison.'

Marianna looked at the date of the article, the fifteenth of February 1946. She took in a deep breath.

"Excuse me!" She stood up and turned to the librarian who looked after the records.

"Yes?"

"May I please have a glass of water?"

"Certainly. Have you found what you were looking for?"

"Yes, but I wonder whether you can help me. Have you any details on a Jurgen Müller? He was a member of the Gestapo in Paris."

"I'll check."

Marianna sat waiting for the woman to come back. She was staggered by what she had read. Her father's best friend had been a traitor. He had collaborated with the enemy right under her father's nose. He had betrayed him. She suddenly hated him. Her sudden anger then turned to sadness. She felt a lump in her throat as she let her mind go back to those dark days at the Velodrome – days that she had forced to the back of her mind so as not to be reminded of the horrors that followed. She began to remember her father as he said goodbye to her at Drancy. She then went on to think about her mother. She remembered how she'd been beaten up in front of her, and how she was dragged away by a French guard. That was the last time she saw them.

"Are you all right?" The librarian asked.

"Yes, yes, I'm fine. It's just that … it's brought back a lot of memories that I thought had been pushed to the back of my mind."

"I know. A lot of people find it very difficult when reading about this period. We have quite a few who come and look up their family war histories through the old newspapers. Are you Jewish?"

"Yes I am."

"Many of the people who come here are." She paused. "Anyway, here is the only piece I can find on a Jurgen Müller. I hope it's what you are looking for.

# 8

Marianna steadied herself as she placed the fiche under the lamp and read the relevant article.

'Gestapo Officer Released Early'. she read. 'Jurgen Müller, a police officer formerly working for the

Gestapo, was released yesterday after serving seven years of his ten-year sentence. He left prison, accompanied by his wife, and will return home to Munich from Lyon where he was held. Müller was convicted for the murder of Roland Bouget ...' Marianna skipped through the piece about the murder since it was merely a repeat of the article printed seven years earlier. 'Reportedly, during his time in prison, Müller has been a model inmate. He has asked for forgiveness for his wartime crimes, in particular for his involvement with the deportation of the Jews from Paris during the summer of 1942. Indeed the chief warden of the prison, said that Müller was a reformed character, who during his time in prison has completed a law degree.'

"Thank you very much for everything. I've seen enough now," Marianna called out to the librarian.

"Good. Will you be back again? Do you want copies of what you have seen?"

"Erm ... I don't think I'll be coming back, but I would like the copies."

"Fine."

Marianna waited for her to come back. She started to pace around, thinking about her next move. She knew what she had to do. She had never been to Munich before. She had never been back to Germany since her liberation from Belsen over fifty years ago. But now she had to go back. She had to find Müller. He was the only lead she had to finding out what had happened to the painting.

# 9

Reinvigorated by the excitement of the investigation she walked quickly out of the building and took the Metro back to her hotel. Staying in the Opera Quarter at The Grand Hotel on the Rue Scribe, Marianna had chosen a place she remembered from her Parisian childhood. Her mother had often taken her there for tea on Saturday afternoons. It was yet another memory that had come back since her adventure began. She picked up the phone.

"Candice? How are you?"

"I'm fine, Marianna. What a day I've had! But enough of that ... Tell me, What happened?"

Marianna told her friend what she had found out. She was so excited, she could hardly contain herself.

"Slowly, Marianna. I can't keep up!"

"Well, the upshot is that I'm off to Munich!"

"What, now?"

"No, don't be ridiculous. I have to find out where he lives and if he would see me before I go. No I have things to do and see here first."

"What like?"

"I want to go back to Avenue Henri Martin, and just look at my old home. I also want to go to ..." Marianna tailed off, finding it impossible to say the word.

"Drancy?" Candice asked, knowing that was the word.

"Yes. I have to go, Candice. It is so strange you know. I have no problems in handling what I went through at Auschwitz, or at Belsen. But here in France I can hardly deal with it. Perhaps it is because it was a French crime, that it was French people who committed these horrors, that makes it that much more difficult."

"Maybe it's about your parents." Candice was not asking her, more telling her to consider her mother and father, whom she had never really grieved for.

"You know, for a young doctor you have a wise head on your shoulders!"

"Tell that to my husband," she replied, smiling into the receiver. "But I'm serious Marianna. You will have to face the nightmare, and it might be tomorrow. After all, it was the last time you saw them."

"Yes, that's true. But I can't really remember them leaving."

# 10

Marianna rose early the next morning. She had ordered a car for the day. She drew back the curtains and opened the windows. A crisp autumn breeze swept into the room. It was a beautiful day. She looked out of her window and saw the magnificent green-roofed opera house. She looked across the Place de l'Opéra towards the Boulevard de Capucines. Nothing had really changed. Even the tea room downstairs, apart from the odd lick of paint, was the same as it had been fifty years ago. Today was a big day. She was looking forward to it, albeit with a nervous anticipation.

The car arrived at nine-thirty. Marianna was

waiting outside.

"Bonjour, Madame Bromberg!" The driver said, opening the door for his passenger.

"Good morning. Have you been told where you are taking me?" she asked in English.

"Yes we are going to Drancy," he replied, taking the hint that she did not want to talk in her mother tongue.

"That's right. I will need you to wait for me. I might be some time. But before we start, I would like to go via Avenue Henri Martin. I know it's in the opposite direction, but it shouldn't take too long."

"No problem, madame. Do you have an address in Henri Martin?"

"No! No, I don't, but I'll know when I see the building," she responded sharply.

It did not take long, in fact just under ten minutes, before the car reached the bottom of Avenue Victor Hugo, and made the sharp left turn into Avenue Henri Martin.

"Do you want me to stop here, or do you want me to continue?"

"Yes, please. Stop here. I need to get out."

Marianna opened the car door and stepped out onto the street she had thought she would never see again. She walked slowly down the beautiful and elegant boulevard. Once again, so little had changed. It seemed so quiet. She looked at the buildings, trying to find a familiar sign. And there it was: the corner building next to the Square Lamartine. The little blue plate with the number '72' on it stopped her in her tracks. This was it. This was her home. She crossed the road and stared at the building, fixing her gaze on the fourth floor. 'Flat ten', she whispered to herself, as memories began to flood back, and familiarity began to take a grip of her. She then crossed back again. She strode purposefully towards the front door, and looked at the names on the buzzers. The family 'Bossuet' appeared to be the new owners. She was about to press the fourth-floor buzzer, but, just as her index finger made contact with the brass button, she hesitated.

It was at this precise moment that all the adrenalin and confidence that she had experienced over the last twenty-four hours suddenly deserted her. All at once she felt no desire to go up to the apartment. It was unlikely, anyhow, that she would be let in; she had no claim on it any more. The government had compensated her for the loss of her home many years ago. But it wasn't just that. She didn't want to go in the old lift, or up the stairs, and see the front door, and then go back into the flat, experiencing a new rush of memories about her parents. She just wasn't ready for it.

She backed away, and then turned around looking for her car.

"Shall we go now?" The chauffeur asked.

"Yes, but I would prefer to go back to the hotel," she said, wiping a tear from her cheek.

"Is there a problem?"

"No."

"Maybe I can get you a coffee. It's only ten-fifteen." The driver looked at his passenger. It was a gamble, but he felt sorry for her. The response was likely to be a rebuke.

Marianna looked at him. He was young, probably about thirty, and swarthy. What he lacked in looks he made up for in charm and sensitivity. They hadn't talked much in the car, but she felt comfortable with him.

"No, thank you. Please take me back to the hotel," She replied, smiling, thus reassuring him that she was not offended.

"OK." He pulled out and drove slowly towards the traffic light, which had just turned red.

"Hey, Herschel! How are you?" A voice shouted out from the car next to theirs.

"I'm fine, Jacques. Are you free for lunch? I am now."

"Yeah! Call me."

The lights changed and Marianna's driver accelerated away.

"Excuse me," she said, leaning forward.

"Yes?" he replied.

"You're Jewish," she said quietly.

He slowed down and pulled over. He then turned around towards the refined and elegant face of his passenger.

"Let's go for that coffee, shall we?"

# 11

Sitting down for coffee on the Avenue Victor Hugo, close to Étoile, Marianna began to tell her driver the story of her early childhood. She told him nothing about the painting, or about the investigations she had carried out at the Georges Pompidou Centre.

"So you are just revisiting. And this is your first time back?"

"Yes. Well, it was to my old home, and it will be to Drancy. I know it seems strange, but I've neither had the strength nor the desire to see it all again. I don't even like to speak in French. I have blocked out my early childhood, even my parents, until very recently. I am sure that if I go to Drancy more things will come back to me which I have blocked out all my life."

"What about Auschwitz? Have you forgotten that?"

"No. Strangely enough I remember everything from the moment I arrived in the cattle truck to the time when I was liberated by the British at Belsen."

There was a pause in the conversation. Harry – his friends called him Herschel, the Yiddish equivalent – looked into the dark blue eyes of his companion. Although sixty-seven years of age, she looked older, but her features remained fine. Tall and slim, she was dressed elegantly in a dark-navy suit. He wondered whether she had a husband or a partner, but decided not to go down that particular road of questioning. Maybe it was too personal, but more importantly it was irrelevant and none of his business.

"You know that you should go there, don't you. One of buildings is still up. There's demand for it to be listed, but as yet the government's done nothing," he finally said.

"Yes ... I know."

"I mean, I am no therapist, but it must be right for you to see it again and confront what might come back to you. Even if it's a fleeting memory of your mother saying goodbye, surely that would be a bonus."

"That's just it. I'm worried that I haven't just

blocked a fleeting memory. It could be a nightmare that is hovering on the edge of the abyss, waiting to attack me." She looked into her cup, and drank the last dregs of the espresso.

"You'll never know unless you go back."

"Are you ready then?" she asked dispassionately.

"What? You want to go now?" He was surprised at the suddenness of the decision.

"Yes. I think you're right. I have to go back ... Just one thing."

"What?"

"When we get there will you stay with me?"

"Of course."

# 12

The black Mercedes made its way out of Paris towards Le Bourget, finally reaching what had been the transit camp at Drancy, five miles outside the city. Getting out of the car slowly, Marianna waited for her driver to accompany her to the main memorial of the site. It was located in front of the only thing that remained from the original camp: the U-shaped building, known as the Horseshoe, where most of the prisoners were interned. Marianna instantly recognised the old building, but directed her concentration to the memorial itself.

"It looks like a woman holding a child," Herschel said, reading the inscriptions on the outer blocks.

Marianna said nothing. She looked carefully at the image, noticing the outer blocks representing gates, in this case the gates of death. Drancy had been known as the 'ante-room of death'. She then looked at the mother and child, with the circular forms at the bottom of the structure which represented the fire and flames engulfing the innocent victims.

Walking back down the steps, and behind the monument, she approached the old boxcar located at the end of the rail line. She hesitated before going inside the wagon. The memories of the camp were now beginning to flood back, but not in any chronological, or sequential, order. Faces appeared, and noises were heard, but little at all made any sense.

She retreated from the boxcar, and turned towards the horseshoe building. Built in the early thirties for cheap accommodation, its purpose remained unchanged. As she came up close to the building she suddenly froze. She quickly turned around.

"What?! What is it?" Herschel asked, slightly alarmed.

"I don't know … this is where something happened." Marianna said, pointing to the open space in front of her.

"What though? What happened here?" he asked.

Marianna said nothing. The memories were now beginning to take some kind of horrific shape. The shape of her mother's face contorted in agony as she lay lying on the floor being beaten by the French guards; her unconscious body being dragged off out of her sight for the last time. But something was still missing; something that needed to be remembered, but refused to come back. She was staring at the ground, the very place where she last saw her mother. Her mind worked back … and then she remembered.

She looked up at her driver. A tear fell down her cheek. She smiled.

"I'm ready to go back now."

"OK." Herschel whispered, taking her arm and walking her back to the car.

# 13

They arrived back at the hotel.

"Thank you," Marianna said, shaking Herschel's hand.

"It was my pleasure. I hope all goes well for you. If you need anything, or if you want to go anywhere, please call me. Here is my card."

Marianna took his card and kissed the slightly surprised driver on both cheeks. She then went straight back to her room. In life's complex pattern there are certain elements that are neither dominant nor crucial, but are part of the grand design. They are necessary because together they make the whole thing work. Herschel would play no further part in Marianna's life, but without him she would never have gone to Drancy. And if she had not gone back to Drancy she would never have remembered her mother's last words to her.

# 14

"Candice, I'm back. Can you come round?" Marianna asked.

"Oh, hi, Marianna. Erm, let me see. Yes, I can see you tonight. David is going to the States this afternoon. Are you free for dinner?"

"Am I free? Oh, let me just check. Goodness ..."

"OK, enough with the sarcasm. I'll book Le Caprice, and will see you at nine."

"See you there then." Marianna placed the receiver down, smiling.

She walked into the kitchen and poured herself a large whisky. She sat down on the oversized leather chair and began to relax for the first time in three days. Her trip to Paris had been both disturbing and exhilarating. Confronting the past was something she had of course expected. What she could not have predicted was the effect that it would have on her. She needed to speak to her doctor, the ever reliable, and understanding, Candice.

Candice's arrival in London had been a godsend for Marianna. The latter, extraordinarily, did not have a doctor. She had never had one. Since arriving in England after the horrors of the Holocaust she had never experienced a day's illness. After going through what she had experienced over the previous three years, Marianna reckoned that she was not susceptible to any malady. She had had her share of pain and affliction. She was now invulnerable. It was therefore a massive shock to the system when she had woken one morning two years ago with the most unbearable headache and a small rash on the back of her neck. Contacting the local National Health GP, she was told he was away, but that a locum was available to take calls in Soho.

It was the first call that Candice took as a doctor in England. Assuring her patient that she would be there shortly, she almost immediately recognised the symptoms of shingles. Her diagnosis was not only right, but also won her the confidence and respect of Madame Bromberg. After the first visit, Candice was a regular guest at Kensington Court where she would listen to her patient's fascinating experiences. Indeed Candice was the only person that Marianna could speak to. She hadn't found anyone to open up to since her husband James had died of a sudden heart attack ten years earlier.

Since his death, Marianna had lived happily alone. After the initial grief, she had coped with his demise relatively easily. That is not to say that she did not love him, or that she did not miss him. He had liberated her from Belsen as a very young British officer, and she had fallen in love with him from the moment he lifted her frail and typhus-ridden body out of the camp hut. They got married less than three years later, on Marianna's twentieth birthday. He left the army to become a university lecturer at King's College in London. They lived blissfully together for thirty-seven years before death took him away from her. But Marianna was well equipped for death, and the grief she suffered, whilst painful, was bearable despite the loss.

The entry of Candice into her life meant that Marianna had a new confidante to whom she could express her feelings. Candice was astounded by some of the tales the prematurely aged patient related to her. By the time that Marianna had decided to start her crusade, and tentatively reach back to her past, Candice knew as much as anyone could about her patient. What she didn't know, Marianna didn't know either.

# 15

"Well? How did it go?" Candice asked excitedly, sitting down at the table, late as usual.

"Exhilarating and disturbing is the best way I can describe it. Seeing Paris again was no problem at all. Being in the city and walking around was enjoyable, even exciting. Very little was personally familiar. I mean I was only fourteen when I was deported. And when I went to Aunt Beatrice's funeral I hardly spent any time in the city."

"But wasn't it great to see the sights ... and be back home?"

"It is not my home." she said seriously. She paused and looked down at her drink and then continued. "I did very little sightseeing, and that was only at the end of the trip. I really couldn't take it all in. My mind was, and still is, in a complete mess. When I arrived I went straight to the Georges Pompidou Centre in Les Halles. Everything was set up for me as planned." Marianna then placed a plastic file on the table. "Read the articles. I photo-copied them from the fiches."

Candice took the file and read through the articles as quickly as she could. Ignoring the waiter, she

signalled to Marianna to order for her. As she fever-
ishly absorbed all of the information from the
various articles, she became more excited. Marianna
meanwhile, having already ordered, sipped her
Bloody Mary, waiting for her friend to finish.

"Well? What do you think?"

"It's amazing. So what now?" Candice asked,
looking up. "I mean to say, what can you do?
Bouget is dead. You mentioned going to Munich on
the phone. Are you sure you want to confront this
man Müller?

"Well, I was sure. Candice, there is so much more
to find out. I was ready to go to Munich and meet
him. Find out whom he was acting for, and why,
and then follow the clues from there. But now I am
not so certain that I should."

"Why? Is it anything to do with what you saw
after you rang me?" Candice was referring to her
trip back to Avenue Henri Martin and to Drancy.

"No and yes! I mean, visiting my old home was
sentimentally rewarding. I had happy times there.
God, they were happy. Even during the start of the
Occupation my father and I used to do so much
together. We even played games like racing each
other up the stairs! There was nothing dark or
sinister locked away in my brain that would
suddenly jump out and frighten me from seeing the
flat. Besides, when the French Government all those
years ago compensated me for the loss of the family
home, I was happy in letting it go. But..."

"But what?"

"But going to Drancy ... well, that was different –
very different." Marianna picked up her drink and
took a large gulp. "It was nothing like I imagined,
and yet the main horseshoe building is still there,

and looks almost identical to what it was. Everything and everywhere seemed so small. I wandered around the whole area, looking at the boxcar, the railway line which linked into Bobigny, and even the building itself. But it was something new that knocked me off my pedestal. There was a stone monument at the front, of a mother holding her child, sandwiched between two slabs representing gates ... the gates of death."

"This was the moment which triggered the memory of your mother? Candice asked.

"Yes." Marianna paused, biting her lip, trying desperately to keep control of herself. "I started to remember everything about that day. At first it made no sense. There was no order to it. It was in flashback form. But then it slowly all came together. By the time I decided to leave ... I remembered everything: getting off the train and being separated from my parents, the noise of the dogs barking, the French guards shouting, my mother screaming and running towards me, and her last words to me, before she was dragged away, beaten continuously by the guards."

"What did she say?"

"She said to look after this, clutching my cardigan, and never lose it."

"Is that it? What happened then?"

"I remember her being dragged away semi-conscious behind another train by one of the guards. I could barely see what happened, but I noticed beneath the train, the guard's lower legs with his trousers dropped around his ankles. I saw the back of my mother's legs, pushed astride as he, presumably ..."

"Enough, Marianna. That's enough!"

"As he presumably raped her." Marianna finished coldly.

"I think you are probably right in not going on with this crusade. As your friend, and more importantly your doctor, I am not sure whether the cost of finding out what happened will be too high for the reward you seek from it. Let it go, Marianna."

"But that's just it, Candice. I can't. It's not just about costs and rewards. Remember, I lived through terror and inhumanity. I'm used to it. The memory of my mother being raped is something I can cope with. It might sound strange, and seem extraordinary, but I saw worse at Auschwitz. But the fact that I can stomach the memories is, in a way, the very reason why I'm not so certain whether I should carry on. The very fact that grotesquely abnormal and subhuman activities can be tolerated is something that I thought I had left behind fifty years ago. I am not sure if I want to go back there."

"I'm not sure either." Candice replied, slightly concerned for her patient. "But tell me, if you did go ahead, what would be your next move?"

# 16

Candice and Marianna drove back down Piccadilly, through Knightsbridge, finally arriving at Marianna's flat in Kensington Court. It was late, well past midnight by the time Marianna pulled down the steps from the ceiling of her bedroom, which led up to the loft.

"When was the last time you went up there?"

"I've never been up there! James always went up for me. Since he died there has been no need to go."

"So, what am I looking for?!" Candice asked.

"A brown leather suitcase. It's very old. It should be towards the back. Be careful," she said as Candice climbed gingerly up the steps.

"Is there a light up here?" Candice called down.

"Oh no. I don't think so."

"Marianna! I need a torch. It's very dark up here." Candice scolded her friend.

"Wait! I'll get you one."

Marianna rushed off to the kitchen, and started randomly opening drawers and cupboards, desperately trying to find a torch. It was to no avail. The only thing she had was a candle. She took it more in hope than expectancy.

"I've only got this," she said, thrusting the candle up at her friend.

"You are joking ... no, you're not joking, are you?" Candice asked looking down at Marianna's shaking head. "OK, pass it to me. I'll light it up here." She took the candle and saucer.

Candice rummaged around in her bag, and eventually found the matches from which she lit the candle, waiting for the wax to drip down onto the saucer to give it support. The flame gave off an unusual amount of light; so much that the entire attic was clearly discernible.

"My God, there's a lot of stuff up here, Marianna. You ought to get someone to clear it out."

"I know."

Candice walked carefully around the stacks of books, the bicycles, the old furniture, finally coming to the pile of suitcases. She placed the candle down on a chair, and then carefully examined the cases. There was nothing remotely brown or very old. She then looked across and saw hanging a British Army Major's uniform. She smiled. She walked over to the hanging garment and felt the coarse material.

"Well?" Marianna's call rudely awakened Candice to her task.

"It's not here!" she shouted.

"Oh, Candice, look again. Nobody has touched it since we moved in here when we got married. It's there, I promise you. Surely you're not going to get a very old sixty-seven-year-old to climb up those stairs." Marianna shouted back, clearly dreading the worst. She really didn't want to go up there.

Candice picked up the candle again, and retraced her steps, searching for the missing piece. She was at the point of giving up, having gone through what she thought was everything.

"No, there's nothing. I'm coming back down." She began to climb down the steps, but just as she was going to blow out the candle, she spotted to her right, against the wall, a dust sheet covering a square-shaped object.

"Hold on. I just want to check something." Candice climbed back up, and pulled the sheet rather dramatically away from the hidden object.

"I've found it!" she screamed triumphantly.

Marianna carefully took the case from Candice on the steps, and placed it down on the floor.

"Well then?" Candice asked, not fully understanding what they were waiting for.

"I haven't opened this case in fifty years." Marianna responded.

# 17

She undid the fasteners, and then slowly opened up the lid of the battered brown case. Marianna then saw for the first time since her liberation a familiar blue-and-white-striped uniform. It was neatly folded, having been laundered, and the yellow star on the front was still clearly identifiable. Marianna carefully lifted up the two pieces of clothing. Candice at once, and for the first time realising its significance, noticed her patient's lower forearm, which revealed the black-numbered tattoo 'A41766'. Marianna's past was represented not only by the transient, yet physical, presence of her concentration camp clothes, but also indelibly by her prisoner number.

There was tissue paper separating the top layer of clothes from the one underneath. This remained untouched whilst the two of them examined the old uniform.

"It's in immaculate condition," Candice said.

"Yes," Marianna replied, staring at the uniform.

"What are you thinking?"

"Oh, er, nothing really ... only that, apart from the cardigan, these were my only clothes for three years. They were the only things that protected me, if that's what you can call it, from total exposure. They became part of me. The reason I've kept them is mainly a sentimental attachment. It's hard to explain." Marianna lifted the uniform to her cheek.

"No, I understand completely. But what about the cardigan?"

"Wait! You're so impatient. It's under here." Marianna said, lifting the hitherto undisturbed white tissue from the case.

And there it was. Just like the uniform, the cardigan had been laundered, folded, and placed immaculately in the case. Marianna did not know quite what to do next. The grey garment, which had miraculously survived both Auschwitz and Belsen through both sheer luck and pure chance had not changed. It had been her saviour in the winters, particularly in December 1944 when she was forced onto an open truck and transported, exposed to the elements from Poland to Germany.

Marianna picked the garment carefully out of the case. She laid it out on the floor.

"Well? What now?" Candice asked.

"I don't know! My mother just told me to keep this. She didn't say anything else. She was dragged off." Marianna got up and walked away.

"Hold on. There must be something here. She must have had a reason." Candice picked up the cardigan. Despite those cold winter days of continuous use, it was very thick wool, which had survived remarkably well. She ran her fingers around the seams and the hems. Then finally, around the collar, her long fingers sensed an additional thickness. She stopped, and then repeated the action, trying to control her excitement.

"Marianna! Quickly! Come here."

"What? What is it?"

"Feel this." Candice handed the cardigan over to Marianna, pointing to the collar.

"God, what is that? It's definitely something. I'll get a knife." Marianna hurried out of the room.

# 18

Marianna cut open the collar of the garment. Although looking in immaculate condition, and handled with such care, the cardigan showed its age as the knife sliced through the stitching as if it were going through butter. The small hitherto unnoticed pocket opened up, the stitching completely falling apart. There resting on the cloth was a folded piece of paper. Browned and frayed, it was clearly very fragile.

"Just be careful. It looks like its going to fall apart," Candice said, holding back Marianna's arm just as she was about to pick it up.

"What do you want to do then? Just look at it and say 'oh how interesting'?!"

"God, Marianna, you can be so difficult. I was only trying..."

"Yes, I know. I'm sorry. But you could say that this is quite important to me!" She interrupted, understating the case somewhat.

Marianna picked up the note. It had hardened, and at first looked like it could not be opened. After returning to the kitchen to fetch a pair of tweezers, slowly and painstakingly she opened the folded piece of paper. The task was made even more difficult since half of it was stuck together.

"It's no use. When it was laundered the paper got damaged. It's hopeless, look!"

"Come on, give it to me."

Dispensing with Marianna's tweezers Candice's long, beautifully manicured fingernails began the process of unravelling the note. Having opened one

110

part of the note successfully, she decided to detach it from the other. Concentrating now solely on the half that was stuck together, she tried very carefully to open it up without compromising the writing. But it was to no avail. She gave up.

"Let's look at what we've got," Candice said, resignedly holding Marianna's hand.

"It looks like some sort of code. The writing was obviously written in some sort of indelible ink. I remember my father used to have it for marking up and referencing his paintings. He would normally put it on the back of the frame behind the painting. It would be clearly visible from the back. The writing underneath is a mess. It's so faded and smudged, it's barely legible. It means absolutely nothing and was obviously written at a different time since the ink is not the same. Looking at it, I would guess the unopened half will be more of the same. We're going to have to forget the rest and just concentrate on the code," Marianna said, examining the note.

Candice nodded in agreement. The code was crystal clear.

"Does it mean anything to you?"

"No, not at the moment. I need to think.

PBPbegà72AHM99.4.10pourM.MCMXLII,"

she said under her breath. "Candice, perhaps I need to go to bed. I'll be fresher in the morning. I need to let my mind rest ... Wait! 72 Avenue Henri Martin; the '4' must relate to the fourth floor, and the '10' is our flat number. But what about the rest? God knows what the '99' is, and the last letters appear to be roman numerals but I don't know. I haven't a clue what the letters at the start mean. I must be missing something. It looks so obvious ... I must go to bed. I'm sorry, Candice."

"OK, Marianna. Of course. Call me." Candice kissed her patient, and went home.

Marianna retired to bed, her mind swarming with the thoughts. She desperately wanted to work out the code. It was obviously her father's writing, and she was in no doubt that it had something to do with his paintings. She needed more time.

# 19

Over the next two weeks Marianna spent her time wrestling with the code, and going through the Munich telephone directories searching for a Jurgen Müller. This was no easy task. There were hundreds of entries for 'J Müller'. After many attempts, some of which were less than polite, late one evening she heard the answer she was waiting for.

"Allo ... is a Herr Müller there, a Herr Jurgen Müller?"

"Yes, this is him speaking. Can I help?" he said in a heavy German accent.

"Yes. My name is Marianna Bromberg. You don't know me, but would you mind seeing me?"

"What is it about? Are you English? Please ... I need some more information." Müller replied.

"Herr Müller, I do not want to waste your time, and I am sorry if I am not too forthcoming, but I don't quite know where to start. I am not English ...

I am French. I was born in Paris in 1928, and deported in 1942. I am trying to recover something of my past. You have nothing to worry about. I would just like some information."

"Is it regarding my activities in Paris, or elsewhere later in the war?" he asked quietly.

"I am only interested in Paris. It is purely a personal matter, I can assure you."

"Is it about Bouget?"

Marianna remained silent. Müller sighed. He had been questioned so much about his past. In recent years, it had become fashionable to research the Holocaust. Nobody seemed to want to talk about it during the sixties and seventies. But now interest had dramatically risen. He didn't mind. On the contrary, talking about his crimes helped release some of the guilt he felt.

"OK. When would you like to come? I live in Munich," he continued.

"Thank you. When are you free?" Marianna replied.

# 20

Marianna arrived in Munich a month later. It was mid-October. Autumn was already making itself felt in the Bavarian capital. She had booked a room at the Hotel Astoria located in the Schwabing quarter, a minute's walk from Leopoldstrasse. She had picked the hotel not only because of its proximity to the city centre, but also because it was so close to where she was to meet Müller, in the English Garden.

To familiarise herself with the following morning's rendezvous, she immediately set out after her arrival to visit the actual meeting place in the garden, the Chinese Tower. Not in fifty years had she felt so alone as she did here. As she walked that evening around the Kleinhesseloher Lake, listened to the buskers, and watched the horses and their elegant riders, her mind constantly wandered back to when she was last in Germany. The horrors that the Germans committed were never more apparent to her than they were now. The sooner she left the better. Having briefly seen the Chinese Tower, she left the garden and walked back to the hotel.

It was dark by the time she returned to the hotel. She ordered room service, and then went straight to bed. Sleep, however, eluded her. The Fatherland was no father to her. She felt alone, vulnerable, and terribly insecure.

# 21

She turned off the alarm well before it was due to go off. She drew back the curtains and opened the windows. Overcast, but very mild, at least it wasn't raining. She wanted to meet Herr Müller outside where there was air and space, not in some claustro-phobic bar or cafe where she would feel inhibited and anxious. She quickly got herself ready,. packed her overnight case, and went down to reception.

Leaving her case with the concierge, she went into the dining room and ordered a coffee. She had no appetite. Her stomach was swarming with butterflies. She didn't know whether she could go through with it. But she knew she had to. She had come this far, so there was no turning back.

She looked at her watch. It was only eight-thirty. The meeting was due to take place at nine. She had plenty of time. Nevertheless she got up, signed the bill, and left the hotel, telling the concierge that she would be coming back to pick up her case at about midday.

She retraced her steps from the previous night, arriving at the Chinese Tower at eight-fifty. She walked around the structure, and then wandered over towards the green coloured benches and tables which were set up around the Tower. She looked around, not knowing quite what to look for. It had been determined that he would find her. His only instruction was that she should tie a red ribbon around the handle of her handbag. This she had done. She had also placed it on the table so that it was clearly visible.

"Ms Bromberg?"

"Yes." Marianna turned around, startled, suddenly facing a short, squat old man.

"I am Jurgen Müller."

# 22

After fetching her a cup of coffee – he made do with water – he sat himself down opposite Marianna.

"Thank you very much for seeing me Herr

Müller. You guessed right on the phone. I do want to speak to you about Roland Bouget."

"May I ask why?"

"He was my father's best friend before the war."

"But why the sudden interest? It's been so long. Surely something must have happened."

"Yes something did happen. A few weeks ago I was visiting a Picasso retrospective at the Royal Academy in London. Whilst looking at the paintings, I came across one particular masterpiece that belonged to my father. I hadn't seen it for fifty years. Before my family was deported, my father gave Roland Bouget the picture for safe keeping until the war was over."

"Go on." Müller said, although Marianna needed no prompting.

"Naturally, I immediately made enquiries to find out where the painting came from, and who owned it. All I found out was that it was given to the exhibition by the Schmidt family, through a dealer in Heidelberg. Before going down that route, I thought I should find out more on Monsieur Bouget. I contacted the public records office at the Pompidou Centre in Paris, who supplied all the relevant information. Obviously that has led me to you."

Müller leaned forward, his hands and forearms resting on the table. He looked into Marianna's eyes.

"You look much older than your sixty-seven years," he said insensitively, but without meaning to give offence.

"Two years at Auschwitz and six months at Belsen doesn't keep you young."

"I am sure. It was a terrible time. My role in the Gestapo was mainly taken up with the French Resistance...."

116

"Herr Müller, I'm really not interested in your role during the war. I am not looking for revenge. Please don't excuse yourself; everybody was guilty, but I don't want an apology. All I want is my painting. Now can you help me?"

"Yes, I can. I remember at the time I was doing a favour for a friend. He was a low-ranking SS officer who had asked me to his office one summer afternoon, just after the first major round-up of the Jews. He wanted me to kill a collaborator named Bouget. I needed the money. It was nothing unusual in those days."

"But he wasn't a Resistance fighter. He was a collaborator. Didn't you think it strange that he wanted him killed?"

"Murder was the order of the day. It didn't matter who you were. It was a lawless society. As a member of the Gestapo, I could kill anyone without any real recrimination. Besides, I made it look like a burglary."

"Did the officer at least tell you why he wanted him dead? The trial reports show very little detail."

"Yes, he did. He wanted me to steal a painting for him. A Picasso picture of a beggar. I presume that this is the painting that you claim is yours."

"Yes." Marianna said excitedly. "And did you?"

"Of course. After I killed him I took the painting and gave it to the officer. He paid me extremely handsomely. But I had to keep my mouth shut. Even at my trial I did not reveal the identity of the officer concerned, or any details of the painting."

"Why not?"

"Well, it wasn't because I had given my word to the officer!" He paused, and then continued, "Ms Bromberg, I assume you have heard of the

117

Odessa Organisation."

"Yes, well, I saw the film *The Odessa File* I assume that it was about the same thing."

"Yes, it was. Obviously, then, I don't need to explain to you how powerful the SS still are. After the war I was petrified. You can see from the depositions of the trial how I protected a number of senior SS officers. Ms Bromberg, I am still frightened."

"Can I show you something?" Marianna asked.

"Yes, of course."

Marianna took the coded message written by her father out of her bag and placed it on the table.

"It looks like a code of some sort. You obviously have no idea, do you?" he said, looking at the script.

"Well, I have worked out that part of the code relates to my address at flat 10, on the 4th floor at number 72, Avenue Henri Martin. I am also sure that it was written by my father just before we were deported. The ink is indelible; he used it to reference his paintings. Did you see anything like this on the back of the frame?"

"No, not that I can remember. It's such a long time ago. I certainly don't recognise anything, but looking at it now surely the last section means something to you."

"What do you mean?"

"The last characters, MCMXLII are they not familiar to you? Think of them as roman numerals".

"Yes. I thought that they might be. Do you know what it means?"

"Well MCMXLII, in terms of numbers, is one thousand nine hundred and forty two." He looked at her and waited.

"1942!" Marianna shouted. "The year of our

deportation. How could I have been so stupid! It must be my age," she smiled.

"Don't worry, Ms Bromberg. Whilst in prison I had plenty of time to read about all sorts of things. Apart from qualifying as a lawyer, I spent many hours learning languages." He smiled back at her. "Now, let's look at the first part of the code. It must relate to the artist and the work, don't you think?"

"Yes ... well, I suppose so." Marianna felt out of her depth.

"'PBPbeg" – it looks to me as if your father was using a multi-lingual code. It must be "Picasso Blue Period Beggar". Now, if we look at the next section ..."

"Well, presumably 'PourM' is back in French, and it must mean 'for me', 'M' being Marianna. So now we are only left with '99'."

"I haven't any idea what that number means." Müller replied. "You'll have to work that out yourself. I'm sure you'll get there." He sat back while Marianna put the code back in the bag and resumed her questioning.

"The officer. Will you tell me who he was?"

"I haven't revealed his name to anybody. I gave him my word at the time. If he's still alive he would kill me. And if he isn't then Odessa will. He was SS through and through. Committed to the Father-land."

"For God's sake, Herr Müller. It's been fifty years. He would be an old man by now. But if he's alive he might be able to help me. He might be contrite and want to help. I won't reveal my source, I promise. Nobody would know. Maybe he's a reformed man like yourself?" she said, trying to coax him.

"He wouldn't be. I knew him. I heard that he was

sent to Auschwitz-Birkenau, to help organise the mass slaughter of the Jews and gypsies. Those guys are not capable of reform."

"Perhaps I knew him then!" Marianna responded jokingly, knowing that there were thousands like him.

"Perhaps you did." Müller looked down at his glass of water. "His name was Klaus Schleicher."

Marianna dropped her cup onto the saucer. It broke. She stared at Müller in disbelief.

"Are you all right Ms Bromberg? Do you want some water?" Müller was concerned.

"No, no, I'm all right." She paused whilst she opened her handbag, trying to search for a handkerchief. "I was right, Herr Müller," she said, wiping her nose and eyes.

"What about?"

"I did know him. But you can relax. Schleicher is dead."

"How do you know?"

"I saw him kill himself." She got up to leave. Müller followed her.

"When? How?" he asked, but she did not respond.

"I wish you luck, Ms Bromberg," he said finally, with an outstretched hand.

"Thank you."

"If I can be of any further help..." He called out to the fast-disappearing woman.

"You can't!" she called back, her emotions in disarray. The most evil influence in her life, which she had banished fifty years earlier, was about to cast its shadow over her again. If she could face it, Heidelberg would be her next stop.

120

# PART FOUR

## Auschwitz: September 1942

### The Camp

# 1

As the train stopped at the very same platform where a month earlier her father had arrived and been sent to his death, the doors were slung open, and the children were forced out of the trucks. Marianna was one of the first to jump off onto the platform. They were lined up quickly by a large number of guards. The black uniform of the SS was the dominant colour of the ruling tyranny. The children stayed motionless, paralysed by fear as the guards, holding back the dogs, bullied and harried them. The fear was compounded by ignorance. None of the children knew what was going to happen to them, or what they had to do. They remained motionless in the cold of the Polish early autumn.

Suddenly, all of the guards stood to attention as a number of officers approached the platform. Looking carefully at the latest arrivals, the young blond captain walked slowly down the line. He was flanked not only by subordinates but also by doctors.

"Where are this lot from?" the Captain asked the guard.

"Paris, sir".

The group of officials continued their inspection.

"What about this one, Doctor Schumann? She is fully developed." The Captain said, stroking Marianna's cheek and then letting his gloved hand brush her breasts.

The doctor walked towards Marianna.

"Tell me your name, and how old you are," he demanded in French.

"My name is Marianna. I am fourteen years old."

"When did you start menstruating?"

"About one year ago."

The doctor turned back to the Captain.

"She's perfect, Haupsturmführer. Well done for spotting her. You haven't been here long but you certainly seem to be able to pick them! It will be interesting to see how my experiment will work on someone young, and seemingly in perfect order."

"Thank you, Doctor. I will have her immediately transferred to your station in the camp."

"Good. Are there any others here?"

"No, that seems to be it," Schleicher said, looking at the other children.

Taking Marianna aside, he ordered all the other children to follow the guards. The path to death was laid out before them. Marianna was left on the platform. Schleicher looked at her. He walked over to her, and stared into her blue eyes. She was beautiful. He took off his glove, and touched her again; this time his hand did not stop at her breast, but reached under her skirt. She quickly moved away.

"Enough, Captain! I need her now. You can have her back when I have finished."

"Yes, Doctor. I would like her back. Don't do too much damage to her," he shouted.

Schleicher watched as Dr Horst Schumann took his victim to the X-ray station he had constructed in the women's camp. The SS Captain walked back towards the officers' quarters in the camp. His thoughts were dominated by the young French girl. He was captivated by her. He wanted to see her again. He would make the necessary arrangements.

# 2

Marianna was taken to the bleak construction where Schumann's machine was located. The experiments Schumann had started were primarily aimed at the effect of X-rays on the genital glands. He was concentrating on sterilisation through the use of radiation. Many of his victims, both male and female, had died during these experiments. Some had survived, but they were rendered unfit for work on account of the radiation burns, and were sent to the gas chambers.

Marianna was told to undress and was sent to the showers. Schumann went back to his office and prepared the machines for the experiment. The phone rang.

"Herr Doctor."

"Yes, who is this?"

"It's Captain Schleicher. About that young girl ... erm, I think her name was Marianna."

"Yes. The one we picked this morning. What about her?"

"I would like her back after you are finished. I need a maid for my quarters, and she would be perfect for my requirements."

"She's a little young, Captain. I mean, she's not yet fifteen. Surely someone a little older would be more suitable."

"Doctor, can I remind you who you are talking to!"

"Of course! I'm sorry, Captain Schleicher. The only problem is that the girl will be in a bad way once I have finished with her. I mean, ten minutes between two X-ray machines, aimed at her sexual organs, for an adult can be lethal let alone for a mere adolescent."

"That is why I am ringing you, Doctor. Just ensure that you don't do more than is absolutely necessary."

"I completely understand!" Schumann replaced the receiver, and continued his preparations.


# 3


Marianna was led into the room, naked. Schumann directed her to stand between the two machines. The doctor looked at her perfectly formed body. Although only fourteen, she had reached a maturity beyond her age. Physically she was a woman in every sense.

"Now just remain still. It will only last five minutes." Schumann tried to reassure her.

Marianna wasn't going anywhere. Although hardened by her experiences at Drancy, nothing had, or could, prepare her for the brutality she was now enduring. She might have looked like a woman but in reality she was simply still a terrified little girl.

The machines were turned on. The rays were directed towards her genitalia. The pain was excruciating. She remained still, enduring the agony of the radiation burns. After five minutes Schumann mercifully gave the order to stop. Usually he would continue for ten minutes to make sure of sterilisation. He did not want to upset Schleicher, who already was developing a reputation for ruthlessness.

As soon as the machines were turned off, Marianna collapsed and lost consciousness.

# 4

Waking up in bed, she felt the gentle touch of a cold compress on her forehead. She opened her eyes, still under the impression that she was dreaming. Suddenly she sat up, remembering where she was. She struggled with the SS officer, trying to get out of bed.

"Stop it, Marianna. Please, I am trying to help." He spoke to her in French.

Marianna continued to struggle. But it was to no avail. The German was far too strong for her to free herself. Besides which, she felt desperately tired. The radiation exposure had sapped her strength. She was unfit for anything.

"Where am I?"

"You are at Auschwitz Concentration Camp, in my personal quarters. I am Captain Schleicher. I have saved you from certain death. So please, do not do me the disservice of trying to escape. This is your escape, your refuge. If you leave here, you will die."

"Why did you save me?"

Schleicher did not respond. He stood away from the bed, sensing that the crisis of her trying to escape had passed. He looked down at her. She captivated him. She was too naive to realise it.

"You must rest for now. When you have fully recovered, you will be my housekeeper. I have cleared it. You will sleep with the rest of the women in the barracks. Every morning you will report to me at seven-thirty."

Marianna suddenly let out a cry. She began to writhe on the bed.

"What is it, Marianna? What is the matter?

She could not respond. The pain from the radiation burns gripped her body. Schleicher knew that he could do little. She was so young and innocent. But he realised that she must have been tougher than at first imagined to have survived so far. He was certain that she would recover. But it would take time. He would protect her for as long as possible. He was already in love with her.

He walked over to the desk and folded the grey cardigan which she had arrived with, but was obviously not allowed to wear. He had managed to recover it from Schumann's laboratory. As he placed it in the cupboard he noticed the name tag 'Bromberg'. He looked up, still holding the garment. He then looked around at the girl.

"Is your name Bromberg?"

"Yes".

He placed the garment in the cupboard and closed the door, appreciating fully the grotesque irony of the situation.

# 5

Marianna did recover her strength over the next number of weeks. What she did not recover was her fertility. The radiation exposure had been enough to sterilise her. She had no idea at the time that she would never have children. This was partly due to ignorance, but also due to the fact that mere survival was the overriding aim of everyone at the camp, and the idea of conceiving children was beyond imagining, especially for someone as young as she.

She knew that she had a relatively comfortable routine. She saw what was happening around her. The endless train arrivals, the piles of luggage left strewn everywhere, the continuous smoke billowing out of the chimneys, and the devastating starvation that surrounded her. Within six months all of the women in her barracks were dead, and had been replaced by new arrivals. They all came with the same sense of fear and despair. There was nothing she could do or say to relieve them. She simply kept her own counsel and maintained a low profile, trying to avoid attention. She knew that if she could keep her job, she could survive.

Still unsure as to why she had been saved, as maturity began to take hold of her in her sixteenth year, she slowly began to anticipate the real motive behind the captain's actions. It was only a matter of time before Schleicher's staring would inevitably lead to some sort of physical approach. Every morning she would arrive at his quarters at precisely seven-thirty. He would open the door and, making sure the door was closed behind her, he would take her hand and lead her in. In comparison to the other guards he was incredibly generous, giving her enough food, although basic, so that she never had to face the starvation that confronted other prisoners. The work was gentle too. It had to be when she first arrived, given what she had gone through. But after she had recovered, Schleicher ensured that she just did his housekeeping.

# 6

It was in the late summer of 1943, almost a year since she had arrived that her protector turned into a predator. His infatuation was about to give in to lust. This in itself presented an enormous dilemma for the devoted SS Officer. Any kind of intimacy with a Jew was against all the rules in the SS code book. Such a breach did not sit easily with Schleicher. But he could not help himself. He was a prisoner to his sexual desires.

"Good morning, Marianna, and how are you?" Schleicher asked.

"I am fine, sir." She smiled and hurried to the bathroom to get changed. He insisted that she did the housekeeping in civilian clothes that he had 'procured' from those less fortunate.

"Marianna! I have a surprise for you!" He called out from behind the door.

"Oh? And what is it?" she asked, excitedly.

"Come and see!"

She cautiously opened the bathroom door, unable to stop herself from entering the danger zone that she was well aware of. The Captain passed the gift to her. She took it, and unwrapped it slowly.

"Will you wear them for me?" He asked.

"Where did you get them?"

"I have a source in Krakow." He lied.

"They are beautiful! Are they silk?"

"Yes, of course. Now, please wear them for me. Now!" His tone suddenly changed. It was clearly an order.

Marianna took the brown stockings and garter belt back to the bathroom. She knew where he had got them, but she had no choice. She could hardly have objected on moral grounds. There was no morality here.

"Wait! Where are you going? I want you to put them on here, in front of me."

"But ..." she objected.

"But what? I have protected you and looked after you for almost a year. I saved your life. Now you do something for me."

Marianna sat down on the chair, pulled up her skirt and put the garter belt around her waist. She then took one stocking and rolled it down. She placed her foot into the silk and pulled it up to the garter. The fit, with both the reinforced heel and toe was perfect. She repeated the action with the other stocking. She then stood up, put her shoes back on, and looked up. The captain was staring at her.

"Come here!" he whispered gently, beckoning her to come closer.

"Please, Captain, let me get on with my work." Marianna began to cry as she approached him, knowing that any pleading would come to nothing.

"Don't cry, Marianna." He stood up and embraced her. His hands took her face. He kissed her fully on the lips. She tried to move her mouth away from his, but was unable to do so. He kissed her again, this time forcing his tongue inside her. She tried to struggle, but gave up quickly.

He picked her up and carried her to his bed. He unbuttoned her dress, and caressed her breasts. He tried very hard to be gentle. He slowly pulled the dress down, leaving her naked apart from her underwear and stockings. He looked into her eyes. His hands were all over her, along her torso, around her buttocks, and down her thighs and calves.

"Don't be frightened, Marianna I won't hurt you." He started to get undressed.

# 7

Marianna pushed him off her. He rolled over onto his side. She got up and ran to the bathroom. She turned the shower on and stood under it for what seemed like eternity. She cleaned and scrubbed every part of her body. Her revulsion at what she had been through made her feel sick. Three months away from her sixteenth birthday, and her chastity was no longer intact. She heard a knock on the door.

"Marianna, hurry up, I need the toilet."

She turned off the shower, making sure that she was rid of any fluids left on or inside her. She wrapped herself in a towel and opened the door.

"Thanks." He laughed as he proceeded to urinate.

She got dressed, leaving the stockings and garter on the floor, behind the door. She heated some coffee, and proceeded with the daily routine as if nothing had happened. Hoping that this was just a one-off event never to repeated, but fearing that he would expect it daily, Marianna prayed throughout the day that he would feel shame and would refrain from abusing her again. Whilst she understood that she needed his protection for her own survival, and was grateful for that protection, paradoxically she hoped that he would be fatally punished for his crime.

# 8

Marianna's fears proved correct. Schleicher's lust for her was not going to be satisfied by a single episode. Every morning she walked down the path leading to the captain's quarters with the dreaded knowledge that he would defile her. There was nothing she could do. She owed him her life, and if this was the only way out, then she would have to suffer the abuse. They rarely talked, and she was still not completely sure what his role was at the camp. All she knew was that by the early months of 1944 he was drinking more and more. At first it was only in the late afternoon after he returned from work, but then it began happening in the mornings before she arrived. The pressure and strain was getting the better of him.

"It's seven-thirty-five. You are late," he shouted from the bathroom.

"I'm sorry." She quickly got changed.

"Don't let it happen again." He threw open the bathroom door with his gun in his hand, half-dressed in his uniform. "If it happens again I will..." He lost his thread, clearly drunk. He could hardly stand up.

"I'm sorry. It won't happen again. One of the women was very ill in the camp, and I had to..."

"I'm not interested. Now come here!" He dragged her delicate young body towards his, and forced his mouth onto hers.

Managing to free herself, she knew he would not be up to anything approaching full intercourse. She put on some coffee. She did not want him to go out in this state. She could not understand why she felt this curious sense of care for him. The feeling revolted her.

"Here, drink this. You'll feel better."

"Thank you." He took the cup of coffee. "I'm sorry for shouting at you. You know I don't mean it. It's just the pressure I'm under. You don't understand. You don't want to understand."

"What is it you actually do in the camp?" she asked gently, not sure whether she really wanted to know.

"I can't speak about it. When it is over, people will not understand what we have done, or what we have achieved. It will be left for future generations to thank us for getting rid of the parasitic elements of society." He was regaining his composure.

Marianna left it at that, as he got up and walked out. She never broached the subject again, partly out of not wanting to know the full details, and partly out of guilt at being allowed to survive. The guilt of survival would remain with her for the rest of her life.

# 9

Activity accelerated at the camp during the spring of 1944 with the first arrivals of the Hungarian Jews. The liquidation of European Jewry was reaching its climax, with the gas chambers in Birkenau alone suffocating more than twelve thousand souls a day. Marianna was oblivious to the numbers, but became well aware of the slaughter. She had been at the camp long enough to know most of the details. She tried to distance herself from everything, desperate to stick to the routine which seemingly afforded her a protective path. But how long could it go on for? She now hardly saw her master, who was out before she arrived and returned just as she had to leave. She knew at the back of her young mind that it was only a matter of time before she would be swallowed up and exhaled through the chimneys of the crematoria.

It was in the late spring of that year that Marianna's 'protective path' deviated towards danger.

"Marianna, I have to let you go. Things are going badly in the East, and operations to finish the job are running at a maximum. I am not able to keep you." He looked into her eyes. He began to break down, sobbing almost uncontrollably.

She said nothing. She obviously feared for her own life, but there was also an element of relief in knowing that she was finally escaping him.

"I know that you must hate me for what I have done to you, but you must understand that I have saved you." He held her hand.

"Yes, I do," she replied, revealing none of her emotions.

"I have managed to get you a job on the platform helping with the organisation of the arrivals. That way you will be near me, where I can see you and still protect you. It's a new platform we have constructed in the camp itself. Everything is so much more efficient now than when I first saw you. The trains come right into the camp under the watchtowers. It's quite extraordinary, you know." His mind started to wander, lost in a quagmire of grotesque and distorted admiration for Nazi organisation.

"Thank you," she responded. Realising fully what his job was, she got up and carried on with her work. Resigned to death, she realised that her 'privileged' existence at Auschwitz was coming to an end.


# 10


The following day Marianna was officially told by one of the women guards that she would be starting work on the Birkenau platform.

"What is it you want me to do?"

"You will be given your orders when you arrive there. Now go!" the guard shouted back.

Marianna made her way quickly to the platform. The chaotic scenes that greeted her shocked her to the core. A train had just arrived. Thousands of people – men women and children – were standing around with their suitcases waiting for instructions. Marianna went towards the Captain, who was clearly in charge of the organisation of the new arrivals.

"Excuse me, sir. I have been sent here. What is it you want me to do?"

"Ah! You're here. I want you to stand over there and help with the suitcases. All of the luggage must be taken and arranged in order. It will be picked up later." Schleicher turned around and walked back to the selection point. There he joined his commanding officer, Rudolf Hoess, the camp doctor, Josef Mengele, and the senior SS women's supervisor, Irma Grese, who watched the new arrivals go past.

Marianna started to organise the cases with other inmates. Occasionally she would look up and see the horrific selection take place. It was brutal. A person's life was determined by one word, either 'right' or 'left', effectively meaning 'work', or 'the gas chambers' respectively. For the first time she saw her protector in his element. The SS storm-trooper, the fascist fanatic and Nazi mass murderer. He was a monster, beyond Marianna's belief. During that morning she slowly became aware of the guilt that would be her companion for the rest of her life. She had been, and was living on the edge of what survivors call the 'Grey Zone': that philosophical area where an inmate would either survive through protection from a Nazi for some service given, or would live by helping the reign of terror to operate.

Admittedly, one could justify one's survival in the 'Grey Zone' by the fact that one had no choice. Marianna didn't. Working on the platform was not her choice. Nor was being raped by Schleicher. However, that did not stop the guilt from entering her soul. She would never let it go, and it would never let her go.

Every day Marianna reported to the platform, and

137

every day she saw thousands being given the death sentence. Every day she got older, and began to realise and understand the horrific significance of what was happening before her. Every day was a new chapter in the systematic genocide of her people. This was death on the assembly line; it had never been seen before.

# 11

With autumn arriving and the eastern chill of the Silesian winter not too far in the distance, operations at Auschwitz-Birkenau began to slow down. Heavy artillery in the areas around the camp was heard more and more frequently. The Red Army was approaching. The camp guards were becoming desperate. Their behaviour began to change from ordered destructiveness to anarchic drunkenness. The pressure on the defence of the Reich and its protectorates was beginning to tell. Marianna saw the change in her protector one day in October.

A new set of arrivals was being selected in the usual manner. The queuing was taking longer than usual, and Schleicher's patience snapped. Usually so cool and reserved in this setting, he started to shout and scream. But the queue remained unwieldy and slow. There seemed nothing that he could do to speed things up.

Suddenly, with no warning at all, he grabbed the machine gun from a camp guard standing near him. Then he opened fire, killing at least twenty people.

They lay strewn across the platform, and he walked around them, swearing incoherently.

"Thank you," he said calmly, regaining his composure and giving back the gun to the guard.

"Schleicher, you fool! This will slow it down even more. Get the bodies out of the way. What's the matter with you?" Hoess screamed at him, disgusted by the young officer's lack of control.

"I'm sorry, Commander. I will get them out of the way immediately."

He called a group of prisoners over, including Marianna. He oversaw the clean-up. He tried desperately not to catch Marianna's eye, but it was impossible. She never took her eyes off his. Her hatred for him grew, as did the guilt over how she could have slept with him. Finally, when their eyes did meet, he quickly turned away.

# 12

The snow began to fall one morning in early December. Marianna was told to report to Captain Schleicher at his quarters. She knew the camp was being dismantled, and many prisoners were leaving. She feared the worst. He was going to kill her; she had no doubt. All she wanted to do was to get out and join the other inmates, but the 'death marches' taking place were far more lethal than she imagined.

"You sent for me." She looked down. She could not bear to look at him.

"Marianna, thank you for coming. Here, sit

down," he said, ushering her in.

"What is it that you want?" she asked as she sat down. She wanted to get out.

"I wanted to say goodbye. You must go very soon. I cannot help you any more. By the way, I have kept this, your cardigan, for you. You will need it. They will march you a long way." He handed her back the grey cardigan, which he had kept for her; the same cardigan in which her mother had sewn the coded message; the very same cardigan which would save her life over the next few weeks as she was taken across Europe in the bitter winter cold. "I also wanted to ask ..." he paused.

"What?" She said, putting on the cardigan.

"Your forgiveness. I have tried to help. I believe I have saved you. But I know that..." He began to break down.

Marianna was at a loss as to what to do. To have forgiven him and then got up and left would have been the safest option. The Captain was drunk, and extremely unstable. He could hardly stand up, and he hardly made any sense. But she stayed still and said nothing.

"Please!" He begged on his knees.

"No. I cannot," she responded, without a flicker of emotion.

"Then it is over. I must ask you to do something for me," he said resignedly. He sounded lucid for the first time as he got up and took his gun out of its holster.

Marianna quickly got up and ran to the door. She tried to open it, but it was locked. She heard his footsteps get closer and closer. She pulled at the door with all the strength that her starving body could muster, but to no avail.

"Here!" he said calmly.

She stopped pulling and turned around. He stood there, holding the barrel of his gun, the handle being offered to Marianna. She stood still, looking at the gun, and then at him. Then she took it from him. She clasped both hands around it, and pointed the barrel at his head. She began to shake. She tried to stop, but her body would not respond. Then she tried to pull the trigger. Again, the same problem presented itself, but this time her fingers would not respond. She gave in. She threw the gun on the floor and turned to the door. No longer in a panic, she managed to open the door easily and began the run back to her barracks.

"Wait. It's easy! Look!" he shouted.

Running away from his quarters she heard the ringing sound of a single gunshot. She stopped and turned around. Schleicher was lying in the doorway. She was only twenty yards away. The gun was in his hand resting by his side. Half of his head had been blown away by the force of the bullet. She stood there for a moment, and then turned back and ran for her life.

# 13

The dismantling of Auschwitz-Birkenau by the Germans accelerated during December. The Red Army was making rapid advances coming west, and it was literally weeks away from discovering the Nazi atrocities that had been committed in the camps.

The gas chambers and crematoria were blown up, but the evidence of mass murder was not completely destroyed. It would not be long before the world began to hear the word, 'genocide' for the first time.

Marianna, meanwhile, was forced on a march from the camp with thousands of other prisoners. In the freezing cold the prisoners made their way through the bleak Polish countryside. On these death marches many died through exhaustion, starvation, exposure, or through a combination of all three. Some were shot for not keeping up; others were left to die by the side of the roads. There was no letting up, as the German guards harried and bullied them to keep walking.

Marianna somehow kept up with the main group. Keeping herself anonymous, she stayed in the middle of the pack, finding warmth and protection from the other bodies. She was one of the few who was not beaten by the guards, or hit by stones or spat at by onlookers. The only real comfort that she had was the grey cardigan that her mother had given her over two years before, which had been kept for her by Schleicher.

She and the people who were forced to march with her were lucky, in that their destination was relatively near. Unlike many concentration camp victims from the east who had to march across Europe, she and her inmates were taken to Krakow, a mere sixty kilometres away. After two days they reached the main rail terminus of the medieval city. Greeted by the all-too-familiar sounds of dogs barking and guards shouting, the prisoners were herded onto the train. Slightly different from the wagons in which they arrived at Auschwitz, this train consisted of open trucks, better adapted to taking coal or other heavy goods. It offered no protection from the cold and the snow for its passengers.

# 14

For Marianna, the next seven days on board the train were a test of survival. The freezing cold was unbearable. Many died on the train journey; their bodies were tossed out in order to ease the crush, but not before they had been stripped of their clothing. As the train approached its destination at Celle, deep inside western Germany, there was plenty of room in Marianna's truck. In fact, of the forty people who started the journey from Poland, less than fifteen had survived.

Once again they were marched out of the station, and made to walk to another hideous location. This time it was a much shorter trip to their new destination, a thirteen-mile march to Bergen-Belsen. Entering the gates, Marianna saw total confusion in the camp. It was massively overcrowded. People were wandering aimlessly. The organisation, so pronounced and dominant at Auschwitz, was totally absent here. She remained in her group, waiting for her orders. There was no indication when, or from where, they would come.

Then from out of the distance she saw a familiar figure approaching. In SS uniform, with heavy boots, a whip in one hand and a leash holding back two dogs in the other, the woman strode towards Marianna's group. She was shouting orders in

German, in which by now Marianna was fluent. She immediately recognised the woman officer. Experience had taught her over the last two and a half years not to show fear; to stand upright and try not to attract their attention. But this was different. This was Irma Grese. The most infamous of all the female SS guards, she was even part of the 'selection committee' on the notorious Birkenau platform. The frequency with which she attacked defenceless prisoners, often killing them without compunction, was well known in the camps. But for Marianna, her reputation was irrelevant. She had seen her kill many times. She had taken orders from her at the platform. She was certain that the monster would recognise her.

# 15

Grese walked around the new arrivals. She approached a number of them, giving orders to her subordinates, who had gathered round, detailing the work to be done by each of them. She stopped short of Marianna, and stared at her. Despite the hardships and the deprivation that she had suffered, and the filth and grime that covered her face and body, her youthful beauty still somehow found a way to show through.

"You! I know you. What is your name?" she asked, lifting Marianna's head with the handle of her whip.

"Marianna Bromberg."

"Where do I know you from?"

"Auschwitz-Birkenau. I worked on the platform with..."

"Ah! That's right. I remember now. You were Schleicher's Jewish whore. You started young, didn't you." She laughed.

"I had no..."

"Don't answer me back." She lashed her whip across Marianna's face, instantly drawing a line of blood from the young girl's cheek. "He spoke most highly of you. He said that you satisfied him." She was now whispering in her ear.

"I wouldn't know." Marianna responded, shaking.

"Oh, I think you would." She walked around her, examining her. "I must speak to Klaus and ask him about you. I could do with a maid here. To keep my quarters clean from all the typhus and squalor."

"He's dead! He killed himself." Marianna waited for another lashing of the whip in response to her answer.

"Is he? Poor Klaus. He was always weak," she said, without a flicker of emotion. "Anyway, I still want you as my maid." She turned to the guards. "Clean her up and bring her to me." Then she left.

Marianna was led away separately from the rest. As she walked past, some of her fellow prisoners shouted at her, and spat at her, accusing her of betrayal, and of being a whore. She did not respond. There was nothing she could do. She thought that they would probably be dead within weeks anyway. She was right. The typhus, typhoid fever and dysentery would decimate the camp over the next four months, and claim over fifty thousand lives.

# 16

"What would you like me to do?"

"I want you to clean my quarters, serve and wait on me ... just like you did for Klaus." She walked towards her slowly, stroking her cheek gently. "I can see why he liked you so much. When I do my inspections I want you to look after my dogs. Sometimes they come with me, but when they do not you will be responsible. If you fail in your duties, I will..." She walked towards the table and lifted the whip and brushed it across her palm. The punishment was quite clear.

"Is there anything you want from me now, or can I go back?" Marianna was desperate to get back. Grese frightened her more than anybody else she had ever met. She had seen her at Auschwitz, and successfully tried to keep away. But here she was right under her control. A proven violent sadistic psychopath, Grese was not going to let the beautiful sixteen-year-old go. She was her slave; her personal property. She intended to get maximum use out of her.

"Yes you can go today, but report back tomorrow at six-thirty."

# 17

Treated like a pariah by her fellow inmates, and like a slave by Grese, Marianna struggled to survive during those final four months of the war. At first Belsen appeared like a holiday camp in comparison to Auschwitz. This was a concentration camp, not a death camp. But within weeks, with the massive influx of prisoners from the East, the con-ditions deteriorated rapidly. Numbers increased from fifteen thousand in November to fifty thousand by the end of February.

Food became less available, and the prisoners began to suffer from the cramped conditions and the increasing lack of hygiene. The spread of disease became a major issue, as the camp commandant, Josef Kramer, known later as the 'Beast of Belsen', tried to control infection. All the new arrivals were immediately disinfected, but in February the disin-fection facility was out of order. Hungarian Jews arriving at that time brought typhus with them. It soon spread out of control, resulting in a death rate during those final weeks of over four hundred prisoners a day.

Marianna survived primarily due to spending most of the day alone, tidying and cleaning Grese's quarters. Out of contact with the main body of prisoners, she managed to avoid most of the horrific conditions the other inmates endured during the first ten weeks. However, she was not immune. Each night she went back to the barracks, where she slept with the other prisoners, and where she was fully at the mercy of the epidemic. It was only a matter of time before she would be infected. It was in the first week of March, just after her seventeenth birthday that she fell ill with typhus.

Grese refused to let her in when she saw Marian-na's condition. She turned away, not even opening the door. It would be the last time that Marianna would see the 'Angel of Death'. She somehow made it back to the overcrowded barracks, where she would remain for the final four weeks of German control. Semi-conscious throughout that month, she could barely eat or drink anything. By the time the Germans handed over the camp to the British in April 1945, Marianna was at death's door. Weighing little more than six stone, she lay still in the bed, waiting for a saviour. He was not long in coming.

# 18

Major James Osborne Clark was detailed to the women's section of the camp. By today's standards, at the tender age of twenty-six, he was incredibly young to be a major, but during the war it was not unusual, given the death rate of officers in combat. Upon promotion, this quintessential dashing blond British officer assumed control with effortless ease. Educated at Eton, and then Balliol College Oxford where he read modern languages, he was a classic example of what the Establishment wanted when looking for leadership. Faced with a deadly combination of starvation, disease and general confusion, he methodically and deliberately put things in order. It took weeks to sanitise the camp. Despite imposing every possible restriction, and putting the entire area under quarantine, over thirteen thousand

Jewish inmates died in the first four weeks under British control.

However, after this initial setback, those who survived were destined to make it out of this dark tunnel of hell. One of those survivors was Marianna Bromberg. Slowly, under the guidance of the British doctors, She took in the right nourishment and started to put on weight.

It was in the third week after the British had taken control that Major Osborne Clark first noticed Marianna. He was inspecting the makeshift hospitals at the time he came to her bed. He looked at the fragile creature in front of him. Although painfully gaunt, she had already recovered some of her beauty as a result of the recent treatment. He was instantly intrigued by her.

"What is your name?" he asked in French, having been told by the doctors of her origin.

"Marianna. Marianna Bromberg." She paused. "A41766," she said, pushing her arm out to reveal her Auschwitz identity.

"How do you do, Marianna. My name is James. How old are you?" he said, sitting down on the edge of the mattress.

"I am seventeen ... I think. What date is it?"

"It is the fifth of May 1945."

"Yes, then I am seventeen."

"What date is your birthday?"

"The third of March."

"Extraordinary," he muttered under his breath.

"I am sorry, I didn't quite hear you."

"I said it was extraordinary. I have the same birthday."

"Well, how old are you then?" Marianna smiled.

"I am nine years older than you," he replied.

Marianna sat up in her bed, ready to talk openly for the first time in almost three years. She quickly went through her experiences at Auschwitz, and then the horrific journey to Belsen. She talked about Schleicher, and Grese, but said little of Drancy, and nothing of her parents. After twenty minutes of rattling through what had happened to her, she felt exhausted.

"I'll let you get some sleep. I must go on." The Major got up, ready to comfort other inmates.

"Will you come back? I have more to tell you." She looked at him with such intensity that he could not ignore her. Her beauty was clearly evident, notwithstanding her fragile state. She was seventeen years old, but she looked much older. She had been aware since her first days at the camp how men now looked at her. The attentions of Schleicher confirmed her attraction, and not just to the opposite sex, as her experience with Grese proved.

"Of course I will," he replied, taking her hand and looking at her.

He walked away and started talking to the other patients. Marianna looked at him. She had never before experienced the emotions that began to take hold of her now. For the first time in three years she felt exhilarated. She kept staring at him walking around the room. Her excitement began to make her giggle. She hid her head under the blanket so as not to let him see her. She tried to control herself, but was unable to do so. The giggles turned into laughter, and then to tears. Marianna cried and cried. The full emotion of the undiluted evil and hatred that she had been through was starting to come out.

# 19

James could not wait until the following day to see the beautiful creature he had met that morning. He went back to the infirmary later that afternoon, and made his way directly towards Marianna. She sat bolt upright as he approached.

"I'm glad you came back. I wanted to talk to you about so many things I missed out."

"Are you sure? Does it help you to talk about such horrible things? Some of them sound simply unbelievable," he replied. The truth about the death camps had not fully revealed itself at this time.

"Don't you believe me?"

"Of course I do. Tell me more," he replied, smiling at her.

"Her dogs!" she replied, looking straight ahead.

"What dogs? Whose dogs?"

"Grese's dogs. They were the most frightening animals I have ever seen. They were more like beasts. She had trained them like that. I had to look after them. If I made any mistakes, she would whip me. I have encountered terrible people, Major, but..."

"Please! It's James. I insist that you call me by my name."

"OK, James. She was the personification of evil. I still have nightmares about her and the dogs." She looked at him. He was her saviour. He represented goodness, warmth, charm and sympathy. She hadn't seen those qualities in three years.

"You must get some sleep. You need it."

"No! You must tell me a little about yourself."

"Me? There isn't much to tell, I'm afraid."

"Oh, come on. For instance, how is it that you speak such fluent French?"

"I read languages at university. I speak French, Italian and Spanish. At the moment I am teaching myself German."

"It is such an ugly language, I wouldn't bother. James, please tell me your life story."

The young Major looked at the frail patient lying in front of him and began to relate to her a story from his early childhood.

"It wasn't easy, you know, but getting the scholarship to Eton was a real turning point for me. My parents owned a small bookshop in Marlow and could never have afforded to pay for a private education. I realised pretty quickly that I was naturally gifted at languages, and the school really encouraged me. By the time I went to Oxford I was fluent in French and Italian. By the time I left, I was fluent in Spanish as well.

"Then I left in the year after war broke out, and had to enlist. I was just 21. Since then, from second lieutenant now to being a major, I have been fighting the war ... and I have no real desire to discuss that with you now." He looked at her, took her hand, brought it up to his face and kissed it. "Now, you really must get some sleep."

She nodded obediently. Completely in love with someone who seemed to her like a demigod, she would have done anything he asked. It would not be long before he would feel the same way about her.

# 20

The dismantling of Belsen and the evacuation of the prisoners began that summer. Marianna had very few relatives left alive that would even know of her existence. James made strenuous efforts on her behalf to try and find her a refuge. Their relationship had deepened, both now knowing that they had fallen in love. Still innocent in its structure and make-up, James was clearly aware of Marianna's age and what she had been through, and the affair was not consummated. The tragic irony was that she had already lost her innocence two years earlier. But now, when she would have gladly given herself to the man whom she loved, it was he who found it hard to take advantage of the offer.

"It's difficult for me, Marianna. You're still only seventeen."

"Technically, you're right!"

"What do you mean, 'technically'? That's your age, whether you like it or not, Marianna."

"What I meant, James, was that I am a lot older than seventeen in every way. I have seen, and been through, more than most people ever see or do in their entire lives. I have suffered starvation from the age of fourteen, radiation exposure and rape at fifteen and typhus at seventeen. And that's just my physical curriculum vitae – I could start on the mental..."

"Stop it, Marianna. Nothing you have said will change my mind. It's only been two months, and although you've regained your weight, and, God, you do look quite exquisite, the doctors have told me you need more time to fully recover. How could I, knowing how I feel about you, take advantage of you when I am still uncertain whether you are well enough to know exactly what you are doing?"

She took his hand and looked into his blue eyes. She retreated, realising he wasn't going to back down. Besides, he was probably right. How did she know if she was sane or not? After what she had been through she knew that she was still vulnerable. They walked around what was left of the camp, most of it was burnt down in May to contain the spread of disease. She was leaving in a few days, for Paris. A cousin of her mother was going to adopt her and take care of her future. Marianna could barely remember her Aunt Beatrice, but she had no choice. There was nowhere else to go and nobody else to go to.

# 21

Marianna left Belsen, which had now become a refugee centre, for Paris by train in mid-June 1945. The nightmare of Nazi barbarity had finally come to an end. Her ride to freedom had begun. However, her emotions at leaving one of the world's most infamous concentration camps were mixed. It was at the hellhole of Bergen-Belsen that she had met her first love, and what would be her only love. She knew that it would not be long before she saw him again, even if he didn't.

Major James Osborne Clark returned to London

later in the same month. He rented a flat in Kensington Court with monies he had saved up. His parents had by now sold their bookshop and retired to Cornwall. He had briefly told them about Marianna, but had kept the information to a bare minimum.

His relationship with his parents was not a close one. Six years at a top boarding school and then three years at a university meant there was little common ground that they could all share. He respected them, and cared for them, but that was really about it. He now had to think about a career.

He had already decided to leave the army and to take up teaching. He applied to a number of universities, finally accepting a lectureship at King's College in London. This was an ideal post for him, having decided to settle in the capital. But in truth, at this time his career took second place in his priorities. During the following twelve months he regularly wrote to Marianna, following her progress back in Paris. She always replied with enormously long letters detailing almost her every movement.

Marianna did not quite fit into her new life back in her home city. She hardly remembered her Aunt Beatrice, her mother's first cousin. The relationship was fraught with difficulties, neither of them wanting to bring up the painful past. Nevertheless, after a number of months Marianna began to make an effort as the horrific experiences of the past receded with time. She also became aware of the debt she owed to her new guardian. Beatrice was the only one of her family who offered any type of help. It was true that a disproportionate number had been deported, or had died, but there were also a good many still alive who could have taken the responsibility of adopting her. But in the end it was Beatrice who was there when she needed her, and it was Beatrice to whom Marianna would always talk when she needed help, and to whom she would always be grateful.

# 22

Within two years of her return, and after many weekends together, James finally managed to persuade her to come to London.

"Do you think she will mind?"

"Who? Beatrice? No, not at all. She might ask you about your intentions!" She laughed.

"I'll tell her!"

"And what are they?" she asked, anticipating his answer with confidence.

"To get married, of course. I would like to do it straightaway, Marianna. I mean, what is the point of waiting?"

She embraced him. She loved him like nobody else. She could not envisage a life without him. She was sure Beatrice would be pleased for her.

# 23

"You are only nineteen, Marianna! Don't you think you should wait a while?" Beatrice asked, feeling a certain sense of justification.

"What for?" she shouted back.

"Well, for a start, what about university? The place at the Sorbonne to read Art History – suppose you will just pass up on that!"

"Oh, who cares about the stupid course! Beatrice, all I want to do is to be with James. I am only happy when I am with him. I am sure that if things don't work out, the place will still be there."

"Probably. But you are so young. And love ... it's so fickle. You could be making a massive mistake."

"I am young, but you know what I have been through. You know what I have lost. I feel that I can deal with almost anything now. The only good thing about the suffering I have been through is that it hardens you. It makes you understand reality. It puts things into perspective, making you appreciate, and not take for granted, the good things in life. James is a good thing! I love him! I know it. You must trust me."

Beatrice looked into her ward's eyes. She was now a beautiful young woman. She would be a catch for anyone. However, Beatrice knew that she was also wilful and stubborn. Nothing was going to change her mind, so what was the point in trying to argue.

"Well, Marianna, it seems that you have made up your mind." She took her hand, and signalled to kiss her. "You have my blessing!" They embraced, mixing laughter with tears.

# 24

Marianna and James got married the following year. The wedding took place in a registry office in London. It was the happiest day of Marianna's life. Despite not being able to have any children, they both decided not to adopt, and the couple remained blissfully happy for the next thirty-seven years. It was a perfect match.

As the years went by, Marianna drew a curtain across her pre-married life, shutting out both the Holocaust and her youth prior to it. The memory of her parents faded to such an extent that she could barely remember what they looked like. Auschwitz, and with it Captain Schleicher, however, never escaped her. This was an albatross that had hung around her neck throughout her life.

In 1985, at the age of sixty-six, James suddenly died. A heart attack whilst mowing the lawn of their newly acquired retirement cottage in West Sussex cruelly snatched his life away from Marianna. He was so looking forward to retirement and spending time in the peaceful countryside with his wife. For Marianna it was a terrible time; she was inconsolable. The Holocaust might have inured her against most pain, but the loss of her only love dealt a serious blow to her heart. However, she slowly recovered, throwing herself into various art courses. She took comfort in reading, and going to museums, and particularly art galleries, to see the new exhibitions. She also befriended a new person, a much younger woman, who happened to be the locum for her regular doctor.

The fact that Candice was from Paris was a coincidence, but there was no doubt there was an instant rapport between the two of them. Not being allowed to speak French – Marianna never really forgave the countrymen who betrayed her family – Candice nevertheless felt more at home with her patient than with many of her husband's friends. It was in this friendship that Marianna's quest for her painting really took shape, and it was Candice's encouragement that would make her go to Heidelberg to claim her rightful inheritance. However, an unexpected tragedy was the match that lit the fuse.

# PART FIVE

## London: July 2002

### Restoration

# 1

"It's bad, Marianna. I can't lie to you," Candice said looking at the reports from the specialist.

"How bad? How long have I got?" she asked without any real emotion.

"A few months, maybe ... certainly no longer." Candice tried to control her emotions, but was finding it increasingly difficult.

"Will I suffer any pain?" Marianna asked coldly, seemingly quite detached from the gravity of her situation.

"No, we can take care of that." Candice got up and walked around her desk. "Marianna, we cannot cure you, but we can make sure that the time you have left will be comfortable."

"Oh, Candice, don't cry." Marianna got up and hugged her young friend. "Look at me, I'm not crying!"

"You! Think of me! I am the one who's going to be losing someone!" Candice stopped sobbing, and suddenly burst out into laughter, realising how ridiculous she sounded in front of her terminally ill patient.

"Now listen. Seriously, I need your solemn promise. Let me keep my dignity. Don't keep me alive for the sake of it. If I start to lose my mind ... you must let...."

"Stop it, Marianna. I won't let you talk about that."

"Well, I better start making arrangements, then." Marianna stood up. "Thank you, Candice, for everything. You are a good friend. I hope you don't mind, but will you help me arrange my affairs. That reminds me, I'll have to instruct my lawyer!"

"Marianna, of course not. But wait, before you go, there is something I want you to do. I think you know what it is."

"The painting. You want me to get it back, don't you."

"Yes. You have to finish it once and for all. You have to bury the past before ..." Candice stopped.

"Before they bury me!" Marianna smiled. "But, Candice, we've been through this before. When Müller told me seven years ago about taking it for Schleicher, it stopped me in my tracks. It put up an enormous wall that I was unable to climb over. I don't want to go back there and face his family. It's too hard for me."

"I understand, Marianna, I think I really do. But if you don't complete the quest, you will be letting yourself down, to say nothing of your parents."

"What do you mean?"

"Your Mother's last words to you were about the painting. Remember how she talked to you about the cardigan. Your father's last significant act was to write a code for you which obviously relates to the painting. It was their legacy to you. You have a duty to them if not yourself."

"But the code! Listen, if we haven't cracked it by now, we're never going to crack it. The '99' means nothing to me. I can't just go to Heidelberg, and tell Herr Schmidt, whoever he is, that it's my painting and I want it back. The code has to be completely broken."

"Forget the '99'. You've almost broken it. It's just one number. It might mean nothing. What's important is for you to go to Germany, and meet with

Schmidt and tell him your story. He might not even see you, but you have to go. You have to try. And you have to start now, because there isn't much time."

There was a pause in the conversation. Marianna thought about what Candice had said. Memories of her father playing with her in Paris began to return; and then a brutal flash recollection of her mother, screaming and being beaten in front of her at Drancy, and then being dragged away by the French guard. "You're right. I'll make contact. But we need to break that code, and soon," she replied defiantly.

# 2

Marianna returned home that evening in a perversely positive mood. She had eluded death's outstretched hand so many times during her childhood, and remarkably had retained good health throughout her adult life. Indeed, she had hardly known a day's sickness since coming to England. Now, however, the outstretched hand had become a grasping paw which could not be avoided. She was not afraid; in fact she was rather relieved. She had lived a full life, and apart from the war years, a very happy one. As long as she could keep her dignity, and not suffer too much, the thought of death did not unduly frighten her. What was far more scary and intimidating was the prospect of contacting the Schmidt family in Heidelberg, and finding out if they still had the painting, and indeed how they had first acquired it. She only prayed that the Schleicher connection was no longer relevant.

Finding the catalogue of the Picasso exhibition held seven years earlier, she thumbed through the back pages looking for her notes. Although so faded that she could hardly read the name nevertheless, the telephone number of the art dealer who represented the Schmidt family was still legible. She copied it down on her bedside notepad, and put the catalogue back on the shelf. She would wait until the morning before starting on her final quest.

# 3

The alarm went off at eight o'clock, as it always did. Marianna had been awake for at least an hour, but had remained in bed. She turned on the light and reached across to her notepad. Tearing off the piece of paper she stared at the number. She then picked up the telephone and began dialling the number. "00 49 6221..." She read the number out loud as she pushed in the numbers.

"Hello? Is that the Breitner Art Gallery?"

"Yes, it is. Can I help you, madam?"

"Well, actually, I would like to speak to the owner."

"Certainly. Herr Breitner, you mean. Who may I say is calling?"

"He doesn't know me, but my name is Marianna Bromberg."

"Please hold on, and I will see if he is free."

Marianna held the phone tightly to her ear. She could feel the tension rise with every second as she waited for him. It seemed like an eternity, but in fact it was less than a minute, before he finally picked up the call.

"Hello, Ms Bromberg. How can I help?"

"Herr Breitner, thank you for taking my call. I am, what you might say, in an unusual situation – though not unique – which you might be able to help me with. Of course, there is no obligation on your behalf to help me. It is just that you are my first port of call."

There was a pause. Both parties were waiting for the other to either continue or respond.

"Herr Breitner? Are you still there?"

"Yes. What unusual situation are you in?" he responded.

"I believe you represent the Schmidt family, in Heidelberg."

"You mean Rolf Schmidt! Yes, I do. It's no secret."

"I was wondering whether you might be kind enough to arrange for him to meet with me at his earliest convenience."

"Why should I do such a thing? I don't know you! Rolf Schmidt is a very important client, and a family friend. If you want to meet him, why don't you contact him directly? I'm sure he's in the phone book."

"That is precisely why I have contacted you, Herr Breitner. I don't know Herr Schmidt, and I think it would be much more appropriate that any communication came through you."

"I still don't understand. Where did you get my name?"

"A number of years ago Herr Schmidt lent a painting to the Picasso Retrospective at the Royal Academy in London. Your name was given to me as his representative."

"Yes, that is correct. I remember the exhibition. Ms Bromberg, can I make it clear to you now that that particular painting is not for sale – at any price!"

"So he still has the painting in his possession."

"Yes ... but, as I have said, it is *not* for sale."

"You are right, Herr Breitner. I would never sell *my* painting!"

There was silence whilst the art dealer tried to comprehend the final remark. It was an unmistakable acknowledgement that he was well aware what she was talking about.

"Ms Bromberg, am I right in thinking that you believe you have a claim on this work of art?"

"That is precisely what I believe."

"And I presume you have some sort of proof, or evidence, to support this claim."

"Yes, I do." Marianna breathed in hard, knowing full well that the code had to be fully cracked sooner rather than later.

"May I call you back, Ms Bromberg. Later today, perhaps? I would like to talk to my client."

"Of course you may." Marianna gave him her number and replaced the receiver.

# 4

Gustav Breitner was one of the best-known art dealers in Heidelberg. He had built up his business through tapping the rich local population that lived in Heidelberg and its suburbs in the surrounding countryside, along the banks of the River Neckar. But it was Rolf Schmidt who was his most important client. Self-made, and now in his mid-fifties, Schmidt ran a very successful wholesale clothing business. He supplied most of the major retailers in Germany. He was a family man, and he was intensely proud of his wife and three teenage daughters.

He had started taking an interest in art after his father died ten years earlier. His real mother had died in childbirth just a year after the war, and his stepmother had passed away when he was at university. After his father's funeral, Rolf went to the bank where his father had been the general manager for such a long time, and where a key numbered 88 had been left for him to pick up. He opened the relevant numbered box, in which he found the wrapped package which had lain there untouched for over forty years. The painting was then revealed for the first time to its new owner, who, although he knew little about art, nevertheless gasped at its magnificence. He immediately took the Picasso painting, the only thing of real value amongst his father's possessions, to a local art dealer for some advice on its value. It was then that he met Gustav Breitner, who was of a similar age. When the dealer saw the work and explained to him its importance and its value, the clothing wholesaler immediately became a client.

Over the next ten years Rolf Schmidt built up a magnificent collection of modern art. By the time Gustav Breitner received the call from Marianna, he had become the leading modern-art dealer in the region. This was mainly due to his close and loyal relationship with Rolf Schmidt.

During that period, Gustav had always persuaded his friend not to sell the Picasso. He felt that it should be given to museums for exhibitions, and in that way Schmidt would gain a position in the art world as a big collector, with, of course, Breitner as his dealer! However, the client had different ideas. What worried him most was the extremely questionable provenance of the painting. He had no idea when and how his father had acquired the work. Indeed, he had known nothing of its existence until after his father's death, the painting having been kept in a bank safe. It was obvious to him that his father wanted nothing to do with it. This added further to his suspicions.

He tried to investigate the background of the work, but came up against the proverbial brick wall. Even Gustav got nowhere in investigating its past.

"Give it up, Rolf. Nobody could have done as much as you in trying to find out where it's from. Just accept it as a gift, and enjoy it."

"I know. You're probably right, Gustav. But you read about all the treasures and money that were stolen during the war, and I just have this horrible thought that it was stolen from some poor old Jew. In a way, the only reason why I let you take it for exhibitions is in the hope that someone out there might just recognise it, and make a claim."

"You're not serious, are you?"

"Yes, I am. Listen, there is something you don't

know about in my family's past."

"What? What is it?"

"My mother had a son by her first marriage. He became an SS officer. He was one of the butchers at Auschwitz. Yes, he was up there with the worst of them. Now, although I have no concrete proof that this painting has anything to do with him, or the Nazis, I would not be surprised if someone came forward to claim it."

"Was your father a Nazi? Your mother?" Breitner enquired.

"My father was a member of the Nazi party, but he had little choice. The bank at that time made it compulsory for their senior managers to join. But the fact of the matter was that my half-brother was a real monster. I was never allowed to ask about him, or even mention his name, after my father first told me about him. My mother, of course, died delivering me. My stepmother wouldn't tell me anything."

"Well, if I get any calls, I'll ring you immediately."

Gustav Breitner had just received that call.

# 5

"Rolf, it's Gustav. How are you?"

"I'm fine, thanks, Gustav. What's going on in the art world?"

"It's pretty quiet at the moment, actually." He paused.

"Ah, so it's a social chat that you want. That's a bit

unlike you," Rolf said, smiling to himself. He stretched across his desk and took his post out of the in-tray and began to look it over.

"No, Rolf. What I have to say could hardly be described as social."

"Well then, what is it?" Rolf asked, still distracted by his correspondence.

"You know you wanted me to call if anybody asked about the Blue?"

"Yes."

"Well, a woman named Marianna Bromberg phoned. She would like to meet you."

"Oh? Why is that then?" Rolf was still relatively uninterested.

"Rolf, she says she has a claim on the Picasso."

On hearing the word 'claim', Rolf threw the papers onto the desk, and stood up. Suddenly his mind went into overdrive, connecting the name 'Bromberg' with the painting. He immediately jumped to the conclusion that his suspicions had been right all the time. He was sure that the Picasso was stolen, and this was going to be his proof. He felt a surge of elation, and was quite oblivious to the prospect of losing the painting itself.

"What did she say, Gustav? I'll have to meet her. I hope she has proof," he responded.

"What do you mean? You're not going to see her, are you? It's ridiculous."

"Why? Perhaps it *is* her painting. I've always told you I was worried about its provenance."

"Yes, but it's your best painting. It's a masterpiece. Unique and irreplaceable. We will never see its like again. I would just ignore her. There are so many of these Jewish claims for stolen art. Listen, Rolf, you don't really know that it could be stolen. You inherited it from your father. It should not be an issue. Let me handle it."

"No! If the painting is Marianna Bromberg's, then I have no wish to keep it. This is quite definitely an issue, and I have to resolve it. I want you to ring her back, and ask her to tell you why she thinks it's her painting. Then come back to me, and I will then decide on whether I should meet her."

"OK. It's your decision." Gustav replaced the phone receiver. He had a nasty feeling that his client would actually give the painting back to the first claimant who came along. He was right about the first thought, but Rolf Schmidt was only interested in returning it to its rightful heir.

# 6

"Hello, Ms Bromberg, it's Gustav Breitner here. I'm sorry for not getting back to you earlier, but I had to speak to my client, Herr Schmidt."

"I quite understand. Will I be able to contact him?"

"Not until you tell me why you think the Picasso is yours. You must understand, we have many people claiming lots of works, particularly when they are as valuable as this."

"Yes, I understand that fully, but it is a very long story. *You* must understand, Herr Breitner, I have very little time. I have not the strength to be able to tell you in detail about my history with the painting, but I can assure you that I am not wasting your client's time."

"Yes, but Ms Bromberg ... you surely don't expect me to let you speak to Herr Schmidt without some proof, or evidence."

"Herr Breitner, I have physical proof as well as circumstantial..." She was interrupted.

"What physical proof? A contract or a purchase agreement?" He was beginning to worry that his worst fears might suddenly be realised.

"No, no ... it's a code, actually..."

Once again Breitner interrupted. "Oh, please, Ms Bromberg. This is madness. A code? What sort of code? Listen. Neither myself nor my client have time for these games. A code, for God's sake!"

"Wait, Herr Breitner. You don't understand. The code will provide your client with physical proof of my claim."

"I am simply not interested. Please do not waste my time." He was delighted and relieved, that her physical proof sounded like complete nonsense, and he felt confident that Rolf would have agreed with him.

"Herr Breitner, perhaps you could do me one favour before you hang up. I am an old woman with only months to live.

"What?" He was irritated at being compromised into feeling guilty at the thought of this old woman dying.

"Could you mention the name 'Klaus Schleicher' to your client?"

"Who?"

"Schleicher. Klaus Schleicher," she repeated.

"Very well, then. Goodbye." He replaced receiver, confident that it would be the last time he would speak to her.

# 7

Breitner immediately picked up the phone and rang his client back.

"It looks like it's just a hoax!" he said nonchalantly.

"What is?" Schmidt replied, baffled.

"The old lady, Bromberg. She gave me this yarn about her only having a few months to live, and that she had some sort of code that would prove the painting was hers. Honestly, Rolf, in future you'll have to let me decide if these people ring with a so-called 'claim'. I can't keep ringing you every time some old Jew calls. These Holocaust claims are becoming more and more common."

"OK, Gustav, you win. I'll let you decide in the future, but you must promise you *will* tell me if anybody with a valid claim calls. I am relying on you. You know how I feel."

"Good, then that's settled. Now, I would like to show you this beautiful Baselitz drawing I have in the gallery. It is exceptional. When can you come?"

"Oh, I don't know. How about tomorrow at nine? Is that OK?"

"Yes, that's fine. OK, I'll see you then." Gustav was about to replace the receiver.

"Gustav, Wait! Just one more thing."

"Yes?"

"Did the old woman mention anything apart from the code? I mean, did she explain why she thought she had a claim, or who she knew? Was there anything else apart from just this code?"

"No, not really." Gustav reflected back on the

conversation. "Oh, yes, there was a name she mentioned. Let me think, yes, I remember ... Schleicher! Klaus Schleicher."

There was silence at the other end of the phone. Rolf Schmidt held his portable phone against his ear as he got up from his chair and walked towards his office window.

"Rolf? Are you still there?"

"Uh, yes, Gustav. Yes, I'm still here," he replied, his mind clearly elsewhere.

"Well? Is there anything else, Rolf?"

"Yes, there is, Gustav. Arrange a meeting with Ms Bromberg as soon as possible."

"What? What do you mean, Rolf?" Gustav shouted, clearly alarmed.

"Just arrange the meeting, and do it quickly."

"Are you telling me that the painting could be hers?"

"No, I am not." Rolf Schmidt clicked the red button on the phone, ending the discussion. He walked back to his desk with a smile on his face. The albatross around his neck was about to be unburdened by an old lady from London.

# 8

Marianna was sitting on her bed by the telephone when it rang.

"Hello? ... Yes... Of course, but when would he like to meet? ... Yes, that's fine ... I am free then. But where? ... OK, I will meet you at your gallery at ten o'clock next Monday. Thank you ... goodbye."

She sprang from the bed and walked around the three-bedroom flat at least five times. She had not felt this exhilarated in years. The pain that she had begun to suffer, and which had become a problem to the extent that she was already on painkillers, had abated momentarily. She immediately started making the necessary arrangements for her visit in five days time. Picking up the phone, she rang the travel agent.

"I need a flight to Heidelberg, please, Juliet."

"Let me have a look for you, Madame Bromberg ... There are no flights to Heidelberg. You will probably have to fly to Frankfurt. I think you can take the train or coach from there to Heidelberg."

"Fine, well, I'll need a flight on Sunday afternoon to Frankfurt, then, and I'll take the coach. I will need a return on the following Monday, the next day. An evening flight. Will you send the tickets to me as soon as possible?"

"Of course I will. Now what about hotels?"

"I need to be in the centre of town, the Old Town. What do you suggest?"

"Well, the most beautiful and indeed the most famous hotel in the Old Town according to this guide would be the Ritter. It's located on the Hauptstrasse and it seems very comfortable, and fairly reasonable. A single de-luxe room costs 140 euros. Is that OK?"

"Yes, that's fine. My meeting takes place somewhere in the Hauptstrasse, so everywhere will be close by. It needs to be: I haven't got the strength to move around so much." Marianna had already told the people who needed to know about her illness.

"Shall I get you a wheelchair for the airports?"

"Er ... I don't know. I suppose so. It will make things easier." Marianna reluctantly agreed. It would be the first time that she would be treated as a disabled person, and she did not feel comfortable with it. But what was the point of telling these people if she was not going to let them help.

# 9

As Sunday approached Marianna became more focused about the trip. She knew nothing of the Schmidt family and was eager to meet them. Her illness, which was rapidly becoming worse daily rather than weekly, worried her.

"I feel so tired. I hope I've got the strength to go!"

"Listen to me, Marianna. You will be fine. I promise that nothing dramatic will happen over the next couple of days. We've stabilised the condition, and although you're not getting any better the treatment you are getting will certainly keep you going over the next few weeks," Candice replied reassuringly.

"If I can't make it, Candice, will you go for me?"

"It won't come to that. Listen, I would have gone with you, but David is also going away that day, and its Sam's sports day on Monday, and I need to go there."

Candice sat back in her reclining chair and looked

at the old woman in front of her. She looked so old and tired. The cancer was taking hold and she was declining fast. But she was strong, and this mission was important for her. She needed to go not just to give her something to live for in the short term, but also because she owed it to herself and her parents that this painting would return to its rightful owner.

Candice wished that she could go with her, but it was impossible. Her husband, David, was leaving for Paris that same afternoon, and there was no way that her son could run in the dash without one of his parents being there.

# 10

David Paradim looked at his watch. It was four o'clock, and although it was Sunday, and there would be very little traffic, he was ready to leave for his six-o'clock flight to Paris. He had never lost that feeling of anxiety prior to travelling, even though he was on a plane at least twice a month. His business took him to all the European capitals; he was a man very much in demand.

Since he started up his own merchant bank, he had rapidly become one of the leading financiers in the country. His reputation rose rapidly to extraordinary heights, and soon he found himself advising multinationals as well as governments. But still the old insecurities and self-doubt never seemed to have left him. Perhaps that was why he was so well liked. Success had not changed him. He really did mix with the modern-day kings, but he managed to keep his common touch.

"Shouldn't you be going? You've only got two hours before the flight leaves?" Candice asked with a mischievous smile.

"Oh, be quiet. You never know, there might be security problems or traffic!" David replied rather defensively.

"But it's Sunday, and you have no cases. You have a Premier Card, so you don't have to queue, and you have a chauffeur, so you don't have to park." She was interrupted from her sport by the doorbell. It was the chauffeur.

"Just in time," David said, opening the door and giving Alan his overnight hand luggage. "You've saved me from being wound up by her. Candice, just one thing – what time would *you* leave for the six o'clock?"

"With no luggage, etc. I would probably leave at quarter to five ... at the earliest!" She walked over and kissed her husband goodbye. "By the way, who are you seeing tomorrow?"

"Georges Bossuet. He owns a very large film-distribution company. He wants to float it on the Bourse. Now, you know that I am staying at the Plaza Athénée, and I will be on the mobile all the time if you need me. You must let me know how Sam does in the race."

"Can I call you even if you're in a meeting?"

"Yes, don't worry. It's fairly informal at this stage. In fact the meeting is taking place at his flat... God, where did I leave his address? Tracy gave it to me ... Ah, here it is. Yes, it's in his flat at 72 Avenue Henri Martin!" He folded the itinerary and put it back in his pocket.

"My God, what a coincidence! That's where Marianna lived. What flat number is it?"

"Flat ten. Anyway, I'll see you tomorrow night." David kissed her and left. Candice stood motionless as the door shut behind him. She was sure that this was fate. The gods were conspiring, but she had to make sure that the conspiracy was a favourable one.

# 11

Marianna's flight arrived at Frankfurt just as David's was leaving for Paris. Taking the coach, just as her ever-reliable travel agent had said, was the most efficient and the quickest way of reaching the old city of Heidelberg. The drive took her to the station in the centre of town. From there she was picked up by her hotel car. Although it was an extremely short distance, Marianna was not able to walk, particularly with a suitcase.

The imposing Renaissance façade of the Ritter greeted the old woman as she got out of the car. Elegant and beautiful, the hotel is surrounded by the castle, the university, the old bridge and the city hall. It is not out of place in such august surroundings. She immediately checked in and was shown to her first-floor room. It was a small standard room, overlooking the main street of Heidelberg, the Hauptstrasse. She had begun to unpack when her phone rang.

"Candice, I've just arrived. The room's a bit small, but it will do. It's only for one night, and I can't be bothered to change."

"Marianna, forget all of that. You will never guess where David has gone tonight."

"Paris! You have already told me," Marianna replied testily. She was on edge. The following day's appointment was clearly on her mind.

"Yes, but where in Paris?" she said teasingly, not picking up on Marianna's mood.

"Oh, God, I don't know, Candice, but tell me. I just don't feel like playing games right now. I'm tired and would love to go to bed."

"He has a client called Georges Bossuet. He heads up some film-distribution business which is about to go on the French stock market. I casually asked him if I could reach him tomorrow, and where he would be. Marianna, when he told me the street and the address, it seemed like a coincidence, but when he read out the number of the apartment, I just couldn't believe it."

"Well?" Marianna was half-concentrating on the conversation whilst taking some pills out of her washbag.

"Flat 10, 72 Avenue Henri Martin," Candice said in a measured tone.

Marianna's concentration immediately returned. The shock of the information made her momentarily lose the sense in her left hand, which resulted in dropping her pills and glass of water onto the floor. Candice heard the glass shatter.

"Marianna, are you all right? Marianna!!"

"Yes, yes, I'm fine, Candice. I've just dropped my glass of water. Hold on." She sat down on the bed and tried to recover some composure. "That is unbelievable ... what a coincidence! He must tell me what it looks like now."

"Yes, of course he will, but don't you think its fate?"

"Why? There is nothing there any more that can help me. I mean, we haven't lived there for sixty years. It's just a coincidence."

"No, I don't agree. It's more than that. We still haven't completely broken the code, and perhaps he might tell me something that will trigger your memory. I am sure '99' relates to something in that flat."

"Look, it might well do. But I just can't think about it. We have broken so much of the code it might be enough to convince people that it provides enough evidence. All of this, though, is conjecture. I have to see Herr Schmidt tomorrow with Herr Breitner, and go through my life story, as well as telling them about the code. For all we know the code might be irrelevant. It might mean nothing to them."

"Oh, come on, Marianna. Don't be so negative. I'm convinced the code will be the physical proof you will need. You did remember the piece of paper?"

"Of course I did. Now, Candice, I'm tired and I am going to order room service, and then go to sleep. I will ring you after the meeting tomorrow morning. Don't ring me!"

Candice put the phone down having effectively been cut off by Marianna. She was disappointed by the old woman's reaction. However, buoyed by David's extraordinary news, she was convinced that something spectacular was going to happen the following day.

# 12

The sun rose over Continental Europe, sending a searing summer heat across its cities. Paris and Heidelberg were no exceptions. Both Marianna and David were relieved to be meeting in air-conditioned rooms for their ten-o'clock appointments. David arrived at the block of flats located at 72 Avenue Henri Martin, on the corner of the Square Lamartine. He got out of the hotel limousine and pressed the buzzer at the door entrance.

"David Paradim to see Monsieur Bossuet."

"Come in, David. I'm sorry, but the lift is not working. You will have to walk."

The door opened electronically, and David walked into the lobby and towards the staircase. Not knowing what floor flat ten was on, he assumed it was not far up. He started briskly to climb the stairs two by two. Counting as he went up, his pace visibly slackened as he reached the second floor. There was no air conditioning in the common areas of the block, and the heat began to take its toll. After the third floor, he began to sweat profusely. He slowed down even more, as he scaled the final flight at no more than a snail's pace.

As he summitted – for that is what it felt like – he put down his case and mopped his brow with his handkerchief. The door to flat ten was open, with its owner standing at the door laughing.

"It's not that bad, David. I thought you were fitter than that," Bossuet shouted from across the corridor.

"It's over ninety degrees, for God's sake. Do you

know how many stairs I've just climbed?"

He was about to tell his host, but was interrupted by his mobile phone.

"Oh, hi. darling, how are you?" David continued to walk towards his client, and signalled to him that it was his wife.

"I'm fine. Guess what?"

"What?"

"Your son has just come second in the race."

"That's fantastic, darling. Can I speak to him?"

"Well, he's just getting his prize. Can I call you back?"

"Yes, of course."

"Why are you panting?"

"Wouldn't you be after climbing ninety-nine steps?"

"What are you talking about?"

"The lift at Bossuet's block is out of order. I've had to take the stairs. Ninety-nine of them! ... Candice? ... Are you still there?" The phone had gone dead.

# 13

Candice cut David off before he knew it, and began to dial Marianna, who at that point was walking slowly with her walking stick up the Hauptstrasse to Gustav Breitner's art gallery. Although not more than one hundred yards from the hotel to the gallery, for Marianna this was a long walk. However, she had passed up on the hotel car since it was such a beautiful morning. Slowly walking, with the aid of her walking stick, her focus was suddenly distracted by the ringing noise in her bag. She stopped, bent down and placed her walking stick on the ground, and began to search for her telephone. She rummaged around, with too much haste and not enough speed. The ringing stopped just as she found the mobile device. She picked it out of the bag and searched for 'missed calls'.

"Ah, Candice, why now? Oh, I'll ring her after the meeting," she said to herself out loud. She switched off the phone, placed it back in her bag, and continued the long arduous walk to the gallery.


# 14


"Ms Bromberg, I presume?" Gustav Breitner opened the door of the gallery and carefully ushered the elderly lady in.

"Yes, that is right. I must thank you and your client for seeing me at such short notice."

"Not at all. Actually, the gallery is closed today. I am preparing for an exhibition, so I am relatively clear." Breitner was clearly moved by the old woman, who appeared so fragile. He felt a sudden guilt at his insensitivity to the woman's claim.

"Is your client here?" Marianna asked.

"Yes, he is. He will be with you shortly. He's just on the phone at the moment."

Rolf Schmidt was upstairs in Breitner's private office, which overlooked the main gallery where

Marianna and Gustav were talking. He looked through the floor-to-ceiling window and watched the old lady talking. He hoped that this woman would be the rightful claimant, and would thereby relieve him from the burden of possessing suspected stolen art. He left the office and walked down the stairs into the main gallery.

# 15

"Ms Bromberg, hello. My name is Rolf Schmidt. I am sorry to keep you waiting."

"Oh, don't worry. Please call me Marianna."

"Well, Marianna, can we get you a coffee or tea, or perhaps a cold drink?"

"A glass of water would be fine, thank you." Marianna felt suddenly more at ease with the charming Rolf Schmidt. His face soft, his manners polite, and his demeanour gentle, he was the sort of man one could easily trust.

"Now then, Marianna, tell me about yourself, and why you think that *The Young Beggar with his Bowl* is your property." Schmidt leant back and opened his arms inviting Marianna to open up and tell her story.

"I was born in Paris in 1928. My parents were Jewish. The family lived in an apartment on the Avenue Henri Martin. My father was a very successful art dealer. He loved Picasso. One of his clients left him this painting in his will. He was so proud of it. I remember the excitement in the flat when he hung it in the bedroom." She paused and sipped some water.

'As you obviously know, the Nazis occupied Paris in 1940. It was a horrible time. My family was rounded up with thousands of others on the sixteenth of July 1942 in 'La Rafle du Vel' d'hiv'. We were first taken to the bicycle stadium, and from there we were sent to Drancy. I was separated from my parents there. My mother was beaten up in front of me, and then dragged away. I never saw her again. Her last words to me were mostly about the grey cardigan I had on. I didn't understand her at the time, and I had forgotten about it until very recently. I'll come back to that later, if I may."

"Yes, of course. What about your father?"

"I was separated from him at the same time. I know that he was sent to Auschwitz, where he was gassed."

"So you were alone at Drancy?" Rolf was desperate for the old lady to continue.

"Yes, for a few months I remained there with other children. I was then sent to Auschwitz, where I spent over two years of my life facing death. I somehow managed to survive there, not without luck. I was eventually transported to Belsen in late 1944, and remained there until the war was over." Marianna stopped, took a deep breath and took another drink.

"Take your time, Marianna. We have all day if you want," Rolf said reassuringly, noticing the black identity tattoo, A41766, on the forearm of the old woman.

"Thank you, but I am fine. I was liberated by the British in the spring of 1945. The only good thing that came from Belsen was that I met my future husband there; he was a major in the British Army. He actually saved me. I stayed in England and recovered to lead a normal and happy life. We had no children ... I was sterilised at Auschwitz." She stopped and looked at Rolf Schmidt.

"So you made a complete break. You never went back to France," He said.

"Yes and No! Immediately after the war I went to stay with my aunt Beatrice for two years. After that I left to get married. I was still only nineteen. I hardly went back for almost fifty years. The French government of course paid me compensation for my parents' apartment. As far as the paintings were concerned, by the time of the Occupation my father had sold almost all of them, apart from. . ."

"The Picasso Blue," Gustav Breitner interrupted.

"Yes, that is correct. I had actually forgotten about the painting. Remember, I was only fourteen when we were all taken away. My father's best friend, Roland Bouget, was meant to keep it for us."

"What made you remember the painting, then?" Schmidt asked.

"Seven years ago I went to a Picasso exhibition at the Royal Academy in London, and that is where I saw the painting for the first time in fifty years. It ignited all sorts of emotions within me, and led me on an adventure across Europe trying to find out what had happened to it."

"But you said that was seven years ago. Why has it taken so long for you to contact us?" Gustav asked, by now totally enraptured by the old woman's story.

"I first went back to Paris and Drancy, where memories came flooding back about my mother, and her last words to me. This in turn led me back to London, where I found the cardigan which I had kept hidden in an old suitcase. Stitched into the shoulder pad was a piece of paper with a code written on it which will be the proof you need. I have it here, look!"

"Yes, yes, I am sure it is very interesting and will be very important in your claim, but can you tell me more about your quest," Schmidt replied, putting the piece of paper to one side.

"Whilst I was in Paris I decided to look up what happened to Roland Bouget. He was an art critic for *Le Temps*. After a little investigation I found out that he was a collaborator, who had then been murdered. Reading the various newspaper reports I discovered that Bouget's killer was a Gestapo thug called Jurgen Müller. I finally got in touch with Herr Müller, who explained his role in the killing and who he was working for.

"And who was that?" Rolf asked urgently, willing the old lady to tell him more.

"Why do you want to know so much about this? Surely you should examine the piece of paper and review the code? It's my proof."

"Please, Marianna; tell me who Müller was working for. It's very important to me."

"The SS Captain who Müller, and indeed Bouget, were working for was a man called Schleicher, Klaus Schleicher. He was transferred from Paris to Auschwitz, where he oversaw the mass killings. He also..." Marianna tailed off, and began to lose her composure as her mouth dried and the tears began to well up.

"He also did what, Marianna?" Rolf was pushing her now. He knew how close he was to finding out what sort of butcher his half-brother was.

"I was his slave, Herr Schmidt. He provided for

my survival. In return, he owned me. I had to do everything. I was fifteen when he first raped me, and then..." Marianna stopped. She couldn't talk about it anymore.

"Marianna, I understand. But tell me, did he survive the war?" He was now tangibly close to finding out what had happened to him.

"He killed himself. He shot himself at Auschwitz. I saw him lying on the ground in a pool of blood."

Rolf Schmidt sat back in his chair. He took a cigarette out of his jacket pocket. He stared at Marianna. "And that is why, I presume, you stopped your adventure. It was too painful for you?"

"Yes. I had no idea at the time that Schleicher was the man who had stolen my father's picture. It was pure coincidence. I still do not know to this day whether he knew who I was. Anyway, I couldn't go on. It brought back too much. Besides, I couldn't crack the code on the paper. So I dropped the whole thing. That is, until I was diagnosed with terminal cancer a few weeks ago ... but tell me, Herr Schmidt – why the interest in Schleicher? Why don't you look at the code? We can then discuss my claim. I mean, knowing Schleicher and telling you about him doesn't help me without some form of proof."

"Oh, Marianna, you have no idea how strong your claim already is. You see, Haupsturmführer Schleicher was my mother's son by her first marriage. He was my half-brother."

# 16

Rolf Schmidt got up from the table and stretched himself. He looked down at Marianna, who stared at him with bewilderment.

"Yes, I know it must come as quite a shock to you, but when I heard what you had told Gustav, I was also shocked." He paused. "But I was also excited. You see, Marianna, ever since I was left this picture in my father's estate I have suspected that it was stolen. I have been waiting for somebody, probably a Jew like yourself, to put forward a claim. As soon as you mentioned the name Schleicher, I knew that I had to see you."

"But I don't understand. How can you be his half-brother? You look nothing like him."

"My father was married to Helga Schleicher, the mother of the monster who you knew at Auschwitz. She was a decent woman. She was a widow at the outbreak of the war, her first husband having died at the Battle of Verdun in 1916. She was still relatively young when she married my father in late 1945. He had been a great comfort to her as a friend during the war, and also immediately afterwards, when she realised her son was not coming back. She immediately became pregnant, and I was born in 1946. Tragically she died giving birth. In those days having a baby at 48 was very risky."

"Yes, I understand." Marianna said.

"My father brought me up with the help of his second wife, who he married much later. Ten years ago he died and left me the painting. He never told me about it, and nor did I ever find out how he got it, but I was very suspicious, given my half-brother's record during the war. There have been a lot of reports on how Nazi officers looted possessions during the war and then passed them down as family heirlooms. I was convinced, given the lack of provenance, and also by the way my father treated the painting, that it was stolen. You see, you have now provided me with the proof. I am delighted that the painting should go back to its rightful owner."

"Well ... th ... th..." Marianna stuttered, not quite believing it would be so easy. "Thank you so much, Herr Schmidt." She reverted back to a more formal tone.

"Not at all. Gustav, fetch the painting, would you?"

"I will, Rolf, but may I have a quick word in private." Gustav Breitner was not going to let his client give up so easily one of the most valuable paintings in the history of modern art.

# 17

"Are you mad? How can you be so gullible? She has no proof, apart from rambling on about some code which she has not produced. She could have made the whole thing up!"

"How? I saw the Auschwitz number on her forearm. She is definitely a survivor. She saw Schleicher kill himself. She even knew about the gangsters and collaborators who worked for him. Don't be ridiculous, Gustav!"

"Listen, I also believe she is a Holocaust survivor. Don't get me wrong there. But everything else could have been picked up from research. Old newspaper records, public records, history books. She might even be an impostor ... Rolf, I cannot let you give her the painting. She has to provide tangible proof."

"For God's sake, Gustav, you must believe her. There is no way she could be an impostor. It's madness to think that she saw this painting on exhibition, researched it, and found out that it was left to me with no proof of past ownership."

"The onus is on her to prove it. For all I know, she might have been a friend of the woman she is describing, who is now dead. At least let us see this code."

Rolf looked through the glass window of Gustav's office, and saw Marianna on the phone.

"OK, Gustav, let's see the evidence!"

# 18

Marianna pressed '3', thereby deleting the last message left on her telephone. It had been left by Candice thirty minutes earlier, and it had given her the last piece in the jigsaw puzzle. She looked up at the two men walking towards her. She smiled as they approached the table, simultaneously wiping away a tear of joy from her cheek.

"Marianna, my adviser here feels that you must show me some tangible proof that you are the rightful owner. He's probably right. I am so full of guilt about owning this painting that I am probably a little too hasty in trying to give it up. Now what about this code?"

Marianna nodded and smiled. Three minutes earlier the code would have provided telling evidence, but it would not have been complete. It would not have proved conclusively, without any doubt, that the painting was hers. But now, with Candice's vital piece of information, the final part of it had been cracked. All she had to do was to find the markings on the back of the frame and explain everything.

"Here it is!" she said, opening the very old piece of paper with the seemingly complex code. "I know it will mean nothing to you, but let me explain." She placed her finger on the code and went through each letter and number.

" 'PBP' is Picasso Blue Period; 'beg' represents beggar; '72AHM' is my old family address, 72 Avenue Henri Martin; '99' was the number of steps to my parents' flat; I remember those steps vividly. My father and I, during the Occupation, raced up them so many times! Flat number '10' is on the '4'th floor; 'Pour' is for 'M', Marianna, and finally 'MCMXLII', is the year when we were taken away, 1942."

"Extraordinary, but who wrote this? Your father, I guess?"

"My father wrote it in his special marker pen. It's totally indelible. It's the only thing that is legible. You can see that the writing below has almost completely faded and is illegible. I think it must have been written by my mother at a later date, with instructions. It would have made things a lot easier!

The code, as you can see, is multilingual"

Rolf Schmidt was fascinated.

"Now, you should find the markings on the back of the frame somewhere. That is where he usually wrote them."

"Gustav, fetch the painting. I don't remember seeing anything on the back."

"Yes, of course, Rolf. Wait there."

Gustav Breitner went into the storage room and brought the painting into the gallery. Standing it up on the table they examined the back and the frame, but found nothing.

"I'm sorry, Marianna, but it's just not here," Rolf said somewhat disappointedly.

"It must have been scrubbed out," Marianna said desperately.

"I thought you said the ink was indelible," Rolf replied gently.

"Hold on, wait, the canvas here is stitched differently. Can you see?" Ironically, it was Gustav, the one least favourably disposed to letting the painting go, who had spotted the difference.

"Yes, yes, you're right. Careful!" Rolf said as he saw the dealer slowly undo the fragile stitching by pulling the canvas free.

And there it was. In the same handwriting, and in the same indelible ink, there was the code for everyone to see. The incontrovertible proof that the painting was indeed Marianna Bromberg's property. By carefully identifying the painting on the hidden flap of canvas, Daniel Bromberg had protected his legacy for his only daughter. Nobody had even thought of looking there. It had meant that the painting would eventually return to its rightful owner.

Rolf Schmidt walked over to Marianna and put his arms around her. There were tears in his eyes. He fully understood the magnitude and importance of what had just happened. Marianna, too, began to cry. An ironic embrace from the genial and generous half-brother of the monster who had stolen not only her father's picture but her entire family, was a fitting end. It was the end of an adventure; a triumphant outcome to an exhausting seven-year mission.

"To which address shall I send the painting, Madame Bromberg?" Gustav Breitner asked Marianna, smiling, now also enjoying the sweetness of the moment.

"To Kensington Court in London, and as soon as possible, Herr Breitner. I don't have long to enjoy it." she replied with pathos, stepping forward to write down her address in full.

"It will be with you by the end of the week!" Rolf exclaimed, putting his arm around Gustav and patting him on the back.

# EPILOGUE

## 1

The painting arrived that rainy day, four hours before Candice came to give Marianna those much needed painkillers. Although the medication did the trick as far as the pain was concerned, the old woman began to lose the will to live. She had finished what she had set out to do. Her painting was hanging above the fireplace in her flat in Kensington Court.

Marianna Bromberg died one month later. There was no family to bury her, her cousins having lost touch many years earlier. It was left to Candice to sort out the arrangements. She spoke to Marianna's lawyer, who said he would be in touch, since she was named in the will to handle various matters. Candice thought nothing of it, and waited for him to get in contact with her.

## 2

"Mrs Paradim?"

"Yes, speaking."

"David Smith-Jones here, Madame Bromberg's personal lawyer. We need to talk," the clipped voice replied.

199

"Oh, right. I hope everything is OK. I know that Marianna left all the proceeds from the flat and all her possessions to various charities. She told me about them."

"Yes, that is correct. Everything has been distributed in accordance with her instructions."

"Oh, I'm pleased. So you didn't need me then," Candice replied, not quite knowing why the lawyer had phoned if everything had been already carried out.

"Well, it's not quite that simple. I didn't need you to handle any of the arrangements, but you are named in the will ... as a beneficiary."

"Oh, how kind of her. What did Marianna leave me?" Candice asked, expecting something modest.

"Before I tell you, Mrs Paradim, the item she has given you cannot be sold, or given to charity, or lent to a museum, except for exhibition purposes. It..."

"Oh, my God," Candice cried.

"As I was saying, Mrs Paradim, the item must stay within your family, and must be hung in your flat. It must never be given away. Is that clear?"

"Yes ... I understand." Candice said quietly, but quite deliberately, fully appreciating the gesture the old woman had made.

"The item in question is a Blue painting by Pablo Picasso, dated 1901, of a young beggar crouching with his bowl. There is a unique identification mark on the inside flap on the back of the frame, which reads..."

Candice interrupted and repeated the code:

"PBPbegà72AHM99.4.10pourM.MCMXLII."

THE END